THE MOUNTAIN'S CROWN

MACAYLA DAWN

*To the readers who long to be writers — I hope to read your story
one day.*

BEFORE YOU READ

The idea behind The Fated Paths Duology came to me in a dream.

Growing up, I was a big fan of 'choose your own adventure' books. I began thinking of my favorite fantasy series—how they follow the main character making a hard decision after hard decision. I thought, 'What would have happened if they had chosen a different path?'.

The Fated Paths Duology follows Penelope Frey, underestimated seventh heir of Paralia, faced with a choice. Will she travel to Oresteia, her family's opposing Kingdom, and help them find what they claim she stole? Or will she follow her best friend to war, fighting for Paralia's army when that same artifact isn't found? Each book in this duology gives the reader a chance to explore what 'could have been' had Penelope picked the other option. Rather than being left with a "what if", we can experience each life Penelope might have gotten to live.

I believe we are all left with choices, and those choices make us who we are. In the end, who will Penelope become?

This isn't a duology like you've ever read before. I hope you enjoy.

Love,

Macayla

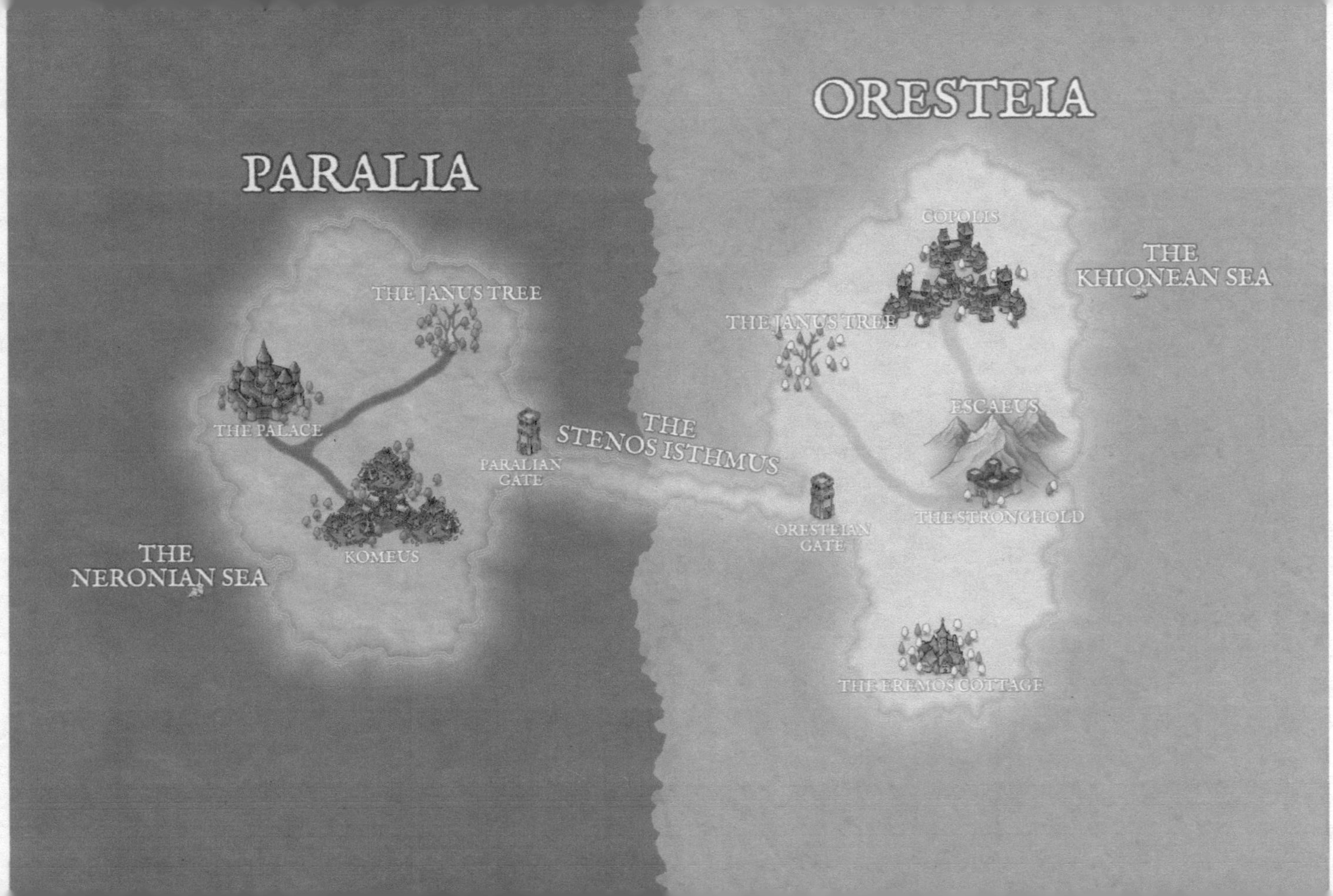

PARALIA
ORESTEIA
THE KHIONEAN SEA
COPOLIS
THE JANUS TREE
THE JANUS TREE
ESCAEUS
THE PALACE
THE STENOS ISTHMUS
PARALIAN GATE
ORESTEIAN GATE
THE STRONGHOLD
THE NERONIAN SEA
KOMEUS
THE EREMOS COTTAGE

PROLOGUE

I could write poems regarding her beauty.

She was the most stunning person I'd ever laid eyes on. The golden touch of her skin seeped into my thoughts like a warm summer day. Her brown eyes held answers to questions I didn't know I needed to ask. Her dark hair wrapped around my dreams like a lover's caress. Her laughter flitted through my mind like a song on the wind.

But she is not mine.

And I will never have her.

CHAPTER ONE

To be drawn to light is to feel alive.

To bask in the warmth of the sun is to feel at home.

Unfortunately for me, Paralia has not felt like home in a long time. Ever since my teenage years, I have longed to experience something new. I have begged the sun to hide, so that I may experience the touch of rain on my skin, or the bite of cold air upon my nose.

And yet, the sun does not give in. Day after day, my bright star shows up and asks me to drown in its rays. My only reprieve is the night sky and the coolness that evening brings.

So here I am, stuck lying on these sandy shores of Paralia, recharging my soul the only way I know how— allowing the sun to soak into my heart and skin.

▲▲▲

"P! I've been looking everywhere for you."

Squinting my eyes open, I turn my head toward the voice coming to sit next to me.

"Cal, don't act like you didn't know I was here." I resume lying on my back with my face toward the sun. Callious and I just chatted not even an hour ago about where I would be spending the day.

Truthfully, he purposefully likes to push my buttons.

All of a sudden, the feel of sand coats my body as he throws mounds onto me.

"Cal!" I giggle and rush upright, trying to spit the sand out of my mouth and brush it off my face. "What has gotten into you?"

"Oh no, I can't believe I got sand on you! I suppose that means we need to take a swim to get it off?" He lifts an eyebrow at me and pastes a smirk on that stupid tan face of his.

Now that I'm sitting up and able to look him in his sea-green eyes, I see that he has shown up to *my* spot in shorts made for swimming.

Of course.

"We have dinner tonight—I can't swim today, and you know that!" I laugh and smack his arm. Cal stands and offers me a hand, but as I gain my footing and take it, he tackles me to the ground and shoves sand in my dark hair. "Callious!"

"Now you've ruined it, Nelly. I wasn't going to, but I am now required to insist that you go for a swim with me. You wouldn't want to head back home plastered with sand, would you?"

Scowling, I push out of his grasp.

"I assume you're expecting me to jump in with my dress on? I'll drown if that's what you want."

"You should know me better than that by now." Cal grabs his messenger bag slung around his shoulder and whips out a deep green two-piece tank and shorts set. "Tailored just for you for these warm waters. You ran out of the Palace before I could give it to you."

"This is stunning—you shouldn't have!" I squeal as I hold the piece up to me. This may be the most beautiful thing I own, with gold detailing on the seams. "Where did you find this?"

"It was Eva's from years ago. She told me she knew of a seamstress who could give it a new life. I just got it back from her this morning."

Grasping the fabric, my smile drops with that declaration. Such a precious gift, and of course, it had to come secondhand through my sister first. I shouldn't be upset, it's still the prettiest set I've ever seen.

"So, does this mean a swim is in order?" He wags his eyebrows at me. Huffing, I roll my eyes in response.

"Give me five minutes to change, and we will race to the waters. And I will not be going easy on you this time."

▲▲▲

Five minutes later, give or take a few, we are shoulder to shoulder facing the Neronian Sea. Even though the name of our sea means cruel or barbarous, it's anything but. I have never experienced warmer, calmer waters than those to the west of Paralia.

I look over my shoulder at my oldest friend. Callious and I have been out here more times than I can count, but for some reason, this time feels different. Maybe it's the way his eyes are shining brighter than normal, or the way he stands so confidently next to me, but I can feel an energy radiating off him that is addicting.

"Ready?" I ask.

"Ready!" He whips his eyes to meet mine. Years of friendship and a mutual understanding reflect in his sea-green eyes. I suppose that could be why looking at the Neronian is one of my favorite views—it reminds me of my best friend.

Deviously, we smile at each other. My heart is pounding out of my chest as I make sure my feet are planted firm in the shifting sand.

"GO!"

We run toward the coastline, elbowing and pushing our way past each other. Years of racing the other means that we have become equal in almost every way, knowing just how fast our opponent is and where they may fall.

My bare feet pound against the soft sand, kicking up small mounds behind us. I surge forward with a burst of energy, my long strides eating up the distance left. Callious matches my pace, determination evident as he pushes himself harder and harder.

My right foot careens into a divot in the sand and I stumble, but Cal is right there to grab my arm and make sure I'm able to keep going. Even though we are competing, he will never let me fall too far behind.

I steal a glance to my right. His athletic build cuts

through the air, pouring every ounce of muscle into his stride.

Our feet meet the cerulean waters as we splash past the shallow part and start swimming toward the waist-deep current. Laughing, he tries to push my head under, but I grab his wrist and attempt to push him over instead.

My body is exhausted, but the race was exhilarating. I pant, my lungs gasping for air. The warm sea caresses my lean figure as I lie back to wash the sand off. Somehow, Cal always knows exactly what I need.

He dunks his head below the surface and flings his dark hair around as he comes back up, coating me in the salty sea. Laughing, I push him further away from me.

"I absolutely won that race. What will I get for being first?"

"You're delusional if you believe you won that. But I suppose that's something I already knew since you still choose to be friends with me after all this time." He winks and dives under as he starts to swim toward me. Suddenly, there are hands around my waist.

I screech as he begins to throw me over his shoulder. "Callious! Put me down!"

"If you insist, Princess." He throws me away from him as if I'm only a sack of vegetables, and into the surf beneath us. I hit the bottom of the sea and rush back up for a breath, only to find him doubled over laughing so hard he can't keep his eyes open.

"I'm not sure why I allow myself to be treated like this by you. Maybe I've had enough!" I shove him with my elbow while wringing out my dripping wet hair.

This is going to take forever to dry now before dinner tonight.

"The day you've had enough of me will be the day I die, Penelope." He smiles as he shoves me back. "Thank you for allowing me to be here today with you, P. I hope I made it worth your while."

I shrug as I say, "I suppose the swim wasn't the most terrible idea you've ever had." Winking at him, I begin to swim back toward the shore where my clothes and responsibilities await. "This has been a fantastic day. Thank you for coming out here."

Halting me, he grabs my ankles and pulls me back in to spin around and face him. Lifting my eyes, I give him a questioning look. "What?"

He sheepishly smiles as he runs a hand through his hair. "Happy birthday, Nelly. I hope I can make twenty-one as special for you as you are to me."

My hand finds my heart, and I give him a sad smile back. "You're the only one who has remembered. Thank you."

He pulls me in for a hug. As we turn back to make our way back to the beach, he flings his arm around my shoulder and kisses the top of my head.

"I know," he murmurs into my hair.

Yes, better than anyone in my life, he knows.

CHAPTER TWO

We hurry back to the Palace, noting the high tide beginning to rise and fall beneath the brick columns that hold my home high above sea level.

One gated wall and fifty-two stairs later, my legs are burning as I rush into my bedroom.

Grabbing a tan-colored towel, I begin wringing my wet strands through the coarse fabric. I put heat on my hair this morning for the first time in a year, but the saltwater always brings out my natural curls.

Huffing in annoyance, I finish drying my long locks as best as possible. If I hurry, I'll have just enough time to change and make it back down to the dining room on time.

My hair may still be dripping as I enter the dining room.

Scouring my wardrobe for something simple to slip on, I quickly find my favorite dress. I'm aware that tonight is important, but I truthfully have no idea what is being announced or what might be going on. The only information I received was second-hand at best through my brother, stating there would be a 'mystery guest'.

I can't help but twirl in the mirror and admire the light pink sheer layer that adorns the maroon skirt. My sleeves are billowed toward the middle but fit tight at my wrists, and my neckline hearts over my chest. I cannot believe my sister, Ana, tired of the dress so quickly. I was ecstatic to take it off her hands.

Slipping into pink flats, I head down the hall to our dining room with just a few minutes to spare.

▲▲▲

I place my hands in my lap as I sit and take a deep breath. It's not easy being without Callious in situations like this, where he cannot be the calm to the storm raging inside of me. Regardless of whether or not anyone else here actually sees me, I know he always does.

My siblings chatter as I look around our dining room. It's not often that we eat in this space together. More often than not, I tend to take my meals to my room for a moment of silence and solitude.

The room is a perfect testament to the natural beauty of our coastal kingdom. It's nestled within the heart of our Palace, overlooking the dark waters of the sea through grand windows adorned with transparent curtains that sway with the bustle of servants moving in and out.

The walls are painted sea-foam green, with white trim as an accent. Seashell chandeliers hang from the high ceilings, casting a soft, warm glow over the polished wooden floors below. Each chandelier is intricately crafted, using seashells from our shore alone.

The focal point of the room is the grand dining table carved from driftwood; its surface polished to a smooth finish that reflects the light. The table is decorated with a pale blue table runner, our plates and utensils coated in gold.

Tapping on a glass, my father rises and begins dinner, capturing my attention.

"Frey, please join me in standing as I introduce our guest for the evening."

Following my family to their feet, my gaze catches on the wide wooden doors that align the wall to our backs. Opening, they present a man with an aura of cool arrogance walking toward us with purpose. His head is held high, and the silver crown atop his head gives off an edge of bitter cold.

This man smiles as he reaches his place next to my father at the end of our table. Looking toward us with ice-blue eyes, I begin to notice many of my siblings' jaws have dropped. It appears the only one holding himself together is Everett, though that is no surprise.

"Thank you for welcoming me into Paralia. It's an honor to set foot once again on your warm coast. Though I do prefer my air with a subtle chill to it," he chuckles.

"You are always welcome here. It has been many years since we last saw each other, so allow me to reintroduce the Frey to you. First, my Queen, Briar." Father takes mother's hand and presents it to this man. His name is on the tip of my tongue, but I cannot seem to place him as my siblings have. There's something in his sharp features that is making me feel as though I've been here before.

"Next, my heir. Prince Everett, please present yourself and be seated."

Everett faces our guest and bows deeply. After carefully finding his seat, he brings his eyes back to our father's.

"The twins, Ana and Eva, please present yourselves and be seated."

They do the same, as is custom. Down the line, my father goes to Finneus, Leila, and Carter, until he reaches me.

"And my youngest, Pen. Please present yourself and be seated."

Trying not to huff in annoyance at the nickname, I follow in my family's steps and make eye contact with our guest, curtsying low to the ground. Bowing my head, I rise and find my seat. Once my eyes are back on my father, all nine of us raise our drinking glasses toward the ceiling in tandem.

"I am the Frey," my father states, still standing.

"And we are the Frey," we respond, taking a sip out of our glasses and placing them back on the table in unison.

"Well, that was a very cute show you put on there, Zannan. Your family has certainly grown in the years we've spent in strife."

I cannot help myself—my eyes grow wide. I have never heard someone speak so casually to my father. Even my mother would not dare use such a tone.

Who is this man?

Father only laughs back as he sits and replies, "Surely you are not still in denial that it was your Kingdom that caused this rift between us in the first place, Kori."

Kingdom.

Kori.

Strife.

Curse the sun above—this is Oresteia's King.

"It's very unfortunate that you do not know how to take responsibility for your actions. I do hope that Prince Everett can steer from your direction in that area should he go on to become King." Kori makes a pointed look toward my brother while taking a drink from his glass. Somehow, he looks as if he is at home here at our table. He lounges back on his seat as if it's his own throne.

Everett clears his throat and looks toward our father for permission to speak. With a subtle nod of his head, Everett declares:

"It would be an honor to take after my King in every aspect once I'm able to receive a crown of my own."

Kori waves his hand in the air and brings it down hard on our table, making me jump.

"Let's cut to the chase, Zannan. I would prefer not to have to stay for dinner if I can help it. Your seafood is…" He pauses to think. "Lusterless, to say the least. Now, give me what has been taken, or give me the girl."

All seven of our heads whip toward my father. My mother sits at his right, and she is the only one who does not look surprised at what is conspiring between these two. Silence overwhelms our space as my father and King Kori stare daggers at each other.

Ana is the one who chooses to break the silence. "My King, if I may, I believe we are all a bit lost regarding what King Kori just proclaimed to us."

My father looks toward her with softer eyes. "Thank you for asking, Ana. Attendants, please clear the room for the rest of the evening."

Feet scurry as our servers and workers race out of the doors as fast as possible. Unfortunately, it does not appear as if we will be eating dinner anytime soon. As if on cue, my stomach lets out an embarrassing growl.

Carter kicks my foot from under the table and sneaks me a pointed smirk. Blushing, I grab my glass and take a slow sip of the fizzy drink, hoping it will curb my appetite for the time being.

Once the doors have sealed and the room consists of only the ten of us, my father stands once more. There's power and authority in his voice and his stance—we cannot help but lean in and listen when he addresses the room.

"King Kori Pan of Oresteia has declared his intentions to go to war on Paralia. He is under the impression that the Frey stole something of extreme value to their Kingdom. Should we not return the item tonight, which I have assured King Kori that we do not have," a pointed look passes between them, "we will then be forfeiting our rights to decline this looming war."

Before any of us can chime in, my mother adds, "Zannan, you must also tell them of the other condition."

My father's shoulders droop ever so slightly as he sighs and continues.

"Because I cannot convince Oresteia's King to reverse his declaration of war, I have negotiated to send an ambassador of Paralia to Oresteia until the season's change to give us time to look for this stolen item.

"This ambassador will give Oresteia insight into Paralia and our systems to help heal the rift that began between our Kingdoms long ago. Should this item not be found at the end of this season, war will begin."

The air is thick with shock as we process the words my father just spoke. Six weeks feels like such a short time in hindsight.

How are we supposed to look for this stolen item when it's clear we don't know what the artifact is?

Kori smirks from his seat. "Don't leave out the best part, Zannan. Tell them who's going back with me."

Our gazes snap back to my father's.

His old, stubborn eyes meet my own while his hand finds my mother's.

"Penelope."

CHAPTER THREE

The dining room erupts in chaos as my siblings go from outraged at finding out I will be living in Oresteia for the next few weeks, to relief in realizing that they do not have to. My father holds up his hand to regain control of the room.

Like dogs heeling to their master, they silence at once.

"Penelope will embark at dawn. The deal is done." He looks from us to Kori. "If you do not want the meal that has been prepared, I can arrange to have something else sent up to your room for you."

"That will be sufficient." Kori holds a hand out to my father. As he releases their handshake, he looks toward me, surveying me from head to toe. I shiver under his cold glare. "You might want to pack a coat."

Turning on his heel, Kori storms out of the room and lets the door slam behind him, knowing full well the level of uncertainty that he left behind.

My father is weary as he sits back down.

"Let's eat."

My stomach churns throughout dinner as my family tries to make small talk regarding anything other than the issue at hand.

Barely able to taste the food before me, I ask to retire to my room much earlier than anyone else. My mother shoots me an apprehensive look, but my father approves my request.

▲▲▲

Back in my room, I collapse on my bed in a fit of disbelief.

I'm traveling to Oresteia.

I leave in the morning.

It's my birthday.

I don't own a coat.

A single knock at my door interrupts my thoughts. Rubbing my face with my hands, I sit back up and face my bedroom door.

The bedroom door I will not see again for weeks.

My father's face enters my line of sight as the door opens. My mood sours more than it was just a minute ago. My arms cross over my chest defensively as I roll my eyes.

"Pen, I know this was shocking to you, but we need to speak regarding expectations I have for you for this brief stint away." He moves forward to my desk in the corner. Tugging at the chair, he brings it to the center of my room to sit in front of me.

"Forgive me for speaking out of anger, King, but I

am not in the mood to discuss the expectations you have for me when my entire world is going to change in less than a day," I snap.

"Penelope, you will hold your tongue. I will empathize knowing this was abrupt to you, but we had no other choice but to send you. You are the only Frey who has no other prior obligations here in Paralia. You know just enough of our systems to lend helpful insight to Oresteia without risking the potential of overstepping in your role."

"Go ahead and say what you truly mean. I have nothing to offer here, and because I know the least of the seven of us, there will be no chance I accidentally say something that could put you or Paralia in jeopardy." I shoot up from my bed and half-curtsy to him sarcastically. "I am so grateful to know that you believe in me and my abilities as a Princess, my King."

Spinning around, I race toward my bathroom, hoping he will take the hint and leave me be so I might process the change before me.

Faster than I've ever seen him move, father leaps from the chair and snatches my arm to hold me firm. I glance sharply at him while I struggle to shake my elbow out of his grip.

Removing his hand, he looks down his nose at me.

Ever the king, rarely my father.

"These next few weeks, you will let nothing stop you from searching for whatever it is that is lost. Here, we will do our part in looking as we are able. The only way to prevent this war is to find what was taken. Should you fail, we all fail. Watch your tongue and watch your back. There's a reason that things have been strained between us and Oresteia for over ten years. If you need anything, find anything, or hear anything, you will write immediately."

Shaking his head, he starts to walk back toward the door. "We are counting on you to do your part. Do not make me regret choosing you."

As he goes to grab the handle, I begin to panic. This may be the last time I speak to him before I am sent off.

"Callious!" I gasp.

He turns around, a questioning look on his face. "Pardon?"

I attempt to regain my composure. "If I may, I would like to request an opportunity to say goodbye to Callious."

My father pinches his forehead between his two fingers in annoyance.

"I will have someone send for him. Is there anything else you would like to *request*, Penelope?" His tone has an edge of bitterness to it, coating the air between us in disappointment.

I allow my steely gaze to look toward him, knowing my father is gone and the King is fully present.

"I'm going to need a coat."

CHAPTER FOUR

Once I am left to my own thoughts and devices again, I realize I don't have any clue how I'm traveling to Oresteia. Other than my apparent need for a coat, I don't know what to pack and what to leave behind.

I stand in the center of my room, the evening sun streaming through the windows. Everything lies in organized chaos as I grab the biggest bag I own and start throwing things in. I begin with practicality in mind, selecting clothing items that are breathable and fit for travel.

I carefully fold and place a long-sleeve gown of deep blue, adding in a pair of matching flats as well. Next, I grab my favorite leather-bound journal and throw from my bed, knowing I will seek both comfort and familiarity in my new space.

Lastly, I place my dagger on top. I'm not entirely sure I'll be able to carry this bag on my own.

Defeated once again, I sit on the edge of my bed.

How did today turn into this?

▲▲▲

As I carefully comb through the rest of my room for necessities—despite the minimal space left in my bag to add anything else—the door opens with no warning.

There's no privacy in this Palace.

Callious looks sheepish as he enters, a hand on the back of his neck.

"Hi," he smiles.

"Hey," I sigh. Just like that, the constant noise in my head empties to nothingness as he comes to sit next to me.

"So, I hear you're leaving?"

"First thing tomorrow. It was news to me, or I would have told you this morning," I grumble.

"What a birthday, huh?" he chuckles, attempting to lighten the mood.

"What a birthday, indeed." Against my wishes, tears begin to form against my lower lashes. Leaning my head on his shoulder, I try to wipe my tears against his rough shirt. "Did you have to wear something so uncomfortable? I can hardly bear to have my head here!"

Laughing, he pushes me off. "No one asked you to lay your head on me, Nel. That's *my* shirt you're sacrificing."

Shoving him back, I begin to laugh. Leave it to him to find ways to reverse the tears that were streaming down my face.

Suddenly, the room quiets. As the minutes tick by, I don't know what to say to him. How do you say a temporary goodbye to a forever friend when you don't know what the outcome will be in just a matter of weeks? Anxiety gnaws at my stomach like the sea to the shoreline.

"Cal, I don't have any special words of parting to offer you. The best I can give is the promise to write if I am able, and my lasting loyalty as your friend."

"If you do not have anything to give, let me give enough for both of us. I have a proposal to make." He leaps off the bed, takes both of my hands in his, and kneels before me on the cold, hard floor.

"Callious, be serious!" I gasp. My wide eyes take in his nervous and sincere demeanor.

My family would never allow such a thing.

He laughs at me. "Not that kind of proposal, P. Although, I cannot help but add that I would give my life to have yours be tethered to mine for the rest of our days. I have loved you since the day you walked into my father's shop with Everett. It has been you and me in my mind ever since."

I smile at this, reminiscing on better days.

It truly has always been him and me.

"I want our hearts to beat in tandem until we die together. I want you next to my side during this looming war, where I can watch your back and you can watch mine. You are the only person I trust with my complete mind and soul. You are the moon to my tide, effortlessly pulling me back into your calm embrace. And so, I ask you this:

"Will you go to war with me?" He pleads, grasping my hands with fervency. "Will you give up your crown to fight by my side?"

The weight of that question does not hit me right away. As it sinks in, I weigh out my two possibilities.

Even though leaving is something I was unable to decide for myself, it's thrilling to think of the new atmosphere waiting for me in Oresteia. All of it is unknown, and that delights me.

But, I swallow. *By going with Callious, I could make this decision for myself. I could have new experiences and still be with someone I know and love, without the burden of being a royal any longer.*

All of a sudden, I am filled with blind rage.

Does he believe running is the only option I have?

"Are you referring to the war I'm attempting to prevent by *going* to Oresteia? If I do not go, war will come immediately. We will not have months to plan, a season to prepare, or days to stand in waiting.

"I am doing something to keep our people and lands safe. You know I love you," I pause, my heart caught in my throat. "But I cannot be whisked away to fight when I can do my best to make sure it doesn't happen in the first place!" I attempt to part my hands from his, but his grasp holds firm.

"Nelly, that's not what I'm saying. Paralia and Oresteia have been at each other's throats since we were nine years old. *Twelve years* we've been in constant strife with them. War is inevitable, whether you find this item or not. You know I believe in you, but to be parted from you would be to sever a limb from my body, *and I cannot go with you.* So please, come with *me.*"

"I cannot just sit back and attempt to believe that. If I leave and abandon my duties, who will go in my stead? Who will go and bid peace between the two Kingdoms, hoping to twine our futures together?

Father already made it clear that I am the *only* Frey who can travel to Oresteia for this long. If I don't go, no one goes."

"But you don't know anything about them!" The strain on his face mirrors the rise in his voice. I have never seen Callious so angry, and his anger has never been directed toward me.

"Just because I was not allowed to be involved does not mean I am of no use!" I scream at him, utterly appalled. "You sound *just* like my father. I may have to take it from him, but I will not take it from you!"

He stands in shock, regret forming on his face. Abruptly, he releases my hands and walks to the edge of the room where my desk sits. Callious runs one hand through his shaggy hair, while the other runs lightly along the notes thrown haphazardly on my desk. Wishes and dreams outline those pages—thoughts I will never speak aloud.

Facing me once more, his breathing calms. "Pen, I'm sorry. I know you aren't allowed in the royal council, and I know it eats you alive to know so little of this Kingdom and the next. I never meant to downplay your ability to do anything that I *know* you are capable of. The thought of you leaving is truly ripping me in half, and I didn't handle it the way I planned when I walked in here. I made you something." He reaches into his pocket and walks back toward me.

"Let me start over. Can we pretend the words that were just exchanged hold no weight over the two of us?" he asks.

I reach for him, nodding and pulling him closer in

front of where I sit on my bed. All anger is forgotten, and I appreciate just how easy it is to be next to him.

"Nelly, I plan to enlist for our Kingdom's army in the morning. I would give anything to have you come with me. You don't need to give me an answer tonight. I would prefer it if you took the time to mull over your options and do what is best in your eyes. I'll be at the Paralian Gate at dawn. If you show up, I will happily twine my arm with yours and never leave your side."

He pauses and cocks his head to the right, pondering. "If you do not, my heart, and this necklace, will be with you wherever you may go."

He pulls his fist out of his pocket and presents a pastel yellow necklace to me, adorned with a beaded chain and a cream-colored seashell.

"Callious… it's… beautiful!" I fluster as he moves behind me.

He turns to place the necklace and clasps it around my neck, and I can feel his hands shaking as the weight of his words sinks into my skull.

A life with him, permanently.

A life apart from him, temporarily.

A new world for me either way.

Once the necklace is secure, I lightly touch the scalloped edge, admiring its soft shell. I stand and spin around to hug him so fiercely that it feels as though my heart and soul are joined with his.

"I will *never* take this off, Callious, no matter what. My soul is so full of you that I could hardly call it my own." I look up at him, meeting his sparkling gaze.

Releasing me with a reluctant smile, he begins to walk out of my room, and my heart pains. I want so badly to call for him to stay with me. I fear that if I did, I would give him false hope as to what we are and what we could be. Regardless, he requires an answer, and I'm the only one who can give that to him.

"Callious," I call, as he reaches for the doorknob. He turns and looks at me expectantly.

"Don't wait for me."

CHAPTER FIVE

THERE WAS NO ONE TO WAKE ME UP.

And there was no coat waiting for me when I arose.

Dawn came with the breaking of the sun over the horizon, relinquishing the slight chill in the air to warm rays upon our palace walls.

Dressing quickly, I pick a deep purple gown with long, tight sleeves, hoping it might be easy to travel in. I put my long hair up into a bun at my nape to keep it out of my eyes as I ready myself to look upon a whole new world.

I grab my heavy bag and survey my bedroom one last time. A gentle breeze is already beginning to flow through my sheer curtains, rustling the pages and flowers on my desk.

My hand finds the soft fabric of my lilac quilt, wishing I had enough room to bring this with me along with my throw. I don't know what my accommodations will be when I arrive, so any small slice of Paralia would be welcome.

But, at the same time, maybe forgoing any items from Paralia is exactly what I need to be excited about my new, temporary home.

Holding fast to my bag's thick straps, I glance up at my tall ceilings, close my eyes, and take in a deep breath.

I'm excited. I'm excited. I'm excited.

Trying to convince myself of that fact, I settle the butterflies in my stomach and move toward the door.

Toward the front steps of my home.

Toward Oresteia.

▲▲▲

I reach our open palace grounds, and there stands King Kori. My brows knit together as I look around for anyone who may be here to send me off.

Not a soul.

Kori's mouth lifts in a smirk as he takes in my confused demeanor. "I guess no one wanted to say goodbye to the forgotten princess, huh?"

I wipe the hurt from my face and look him in the eyes. "I don't *need* to say goodbye to them to know they care for me," I bite back.

"Right. I'm sure that's the case." Breaking eye contact, he begins to walk toward our golden front gate, leaving me behind.

I lengthen my stride to keep up with him, nearly losing my breath in the process.

I shouldn't have packed anything in this bag at all if this is how our trip is going to go.

Reluctantly, I huff, "Forgive me for asking, but I'm not familiar with the traveling procedure for getting to Oresteia. Would you be able to fill in those gaps for me?"

"We will be walking."

I skid to a halt on the sandy path. I should have picked different shoes. "Walking? To Oresteia?"

Walking backward now, he turns to face me and cocks his head in annoyance, "No, not to Oresteia. To the Janus Tree." Flipping his body to face forward, he has not lost a single bit of ground as he continues to walk further and further away from me.

Scurrying, I slip on the shifting sand as I begin rushing toward him again. My sleeves are beginning to itch, and my bun is unraveling in this dry heat.

With sweat dripping down my forehead, I clutch my bag and begin to quicken my pace to keep up with him.

"What is a sun-forsaken Janus Tree?" I exclaim, losing all sense of self-preservation. I no longer care if he thinks I'm not knowledgeable—I have *never* heard of such a thing.

"Please, do us both a favor and save your breath for the journey. I would prefer not to have to deal with you fainting on me. I will explain when we get there. For now, *keep up*."

Mumbling, I clamp my mouth shut and continue to follow him down the hill to who-knows- where. Because our palace must be elevated from the sea, it's a long way down to our city, Komeus. Though, I do not believe that is the direction he is leading me toward.

Not that I would know, apparently.

The rolling hills are filled with paspalos grass, growing stubbornly in our dry, sandy plains. I love watching the grass sway in a slight breeze when Paralia gifts us such a thing. Though it is rare, when we receive a day like that, Cal and I will often go racing barefoot through the fields between our palace and Komeus, just to feel more of a wind at our backs and on our faces.

My heart refreshes at the memory, and I smile as I pick up my pace to match Kori's. All of a sudden, he veers off this path to the left, headed for a small grove of kaluptos trees on the edge of our cliff.

Diving deeper into the trees, I realize I've never been this close to Paralia's cliff edge before. Not being one for heights, I haven't particularly cared what it would be like to stand so close as to hear the roaring waters and survey the jagged rocks below.

A shudder goes through my body at the thought of slipping off the edge, knowing your end is near, and not being able to do anything about it but wait.

▲▲▲

As time moves on, the midday sun beats down on my back. King Kori has not wavered in his speed once. I had not realized the grove went so deep into Paralia, and the kaluptos' small green leaves give zero coverage to the harsh rays.

In front of me, Kori pulls back a large amount of vine hanging from a long kaluptos branch. Gesturing for me to walk through, I do not hesitate to enter the cool shade this pocket in the grove brings.

I spin on my heel, admiring the small hidden cove that has taken form in front of my eyes. As Kori enters himself and drops the hanging leaves from his grasp, the space envelopes us in a cold darkness. On all sides of me, leaves are hanging in strands so tightly woven together that not an inch of sunlight peeks through.

There's a slight amber glow coming from the far wall of greenery adjacent to where I'm standing. Planted in the grass, a tree trunk thicker than anything I've ever laid my eyes on sprouts up out of the ground and towers over us with wide branches.

I reach out, hoping to catch a feel for the radiant color leaching off the bark.

"It's gorgeous, isn't it?" Kori asks from behind, startling me.

I snap my hand back as if burned. "I forgot you were there."

He laughs, moving in front of me to stand in front of the tree.

"This is the Janus Tree. You've never heard anything regarding it?"

I shake my head, feeling ashamed.

He sighs, clearly disappointed. "The Janus tree has been around longer than anyone can remember. For centuries, this has been the route that we have taken to quickly connect our two Kingdoms. A closely guarded secret, only the royal families of Paralia and Oresteia know about this tree.

"The tale of the origin is passed down from generation to generation. We believe that our ancestors were once hostile enemies, and it was here they struck a blood bargain between the two rulers. Clasping slit hands, their blood mixed and dropped onto this dirt, connecting our two Kingdoms forever. One must have royal blood running through their veins, or the stamp of the Kingdom marked into their skin to enter. Even then, the Tree tests your heart's intentions as you move, only letting the trustworthy through."

"How can a Tree know someone's inner wishes? Can it not be swayed by one Kingdom or the other?" I ask.

"The Janus Tree is impartial to both Paralia and Oresteia, as the bargain promised. You will find once we go through that there is no gap between Kingdoms —this tree roots itself in Paralia just as much as it is rooted in Oresteia."

"What do you mean by... go *through?*"

Kori chuckles at me. "Place your hand on the heart of the Tree and you will see."

Hesitantly, I move forward and place my palm upon the glowing center of the Janus Tree. As soon as I make contact with the rough bark, it begins to change and sway around my hand, creating an opening right in the middle.

With a wooden door tucked inside.

I gasp. I have never seen such a thing happen, especially not in Paralia.

"How...?"

"As I said, only those approved with royal blood or markings may enter. Once we go through, the door will emerge on the other side of this tree into Oresteia. As we exit over there, this door will once again be covered by the hull of the tree."

"And if someone's intentions are not true? What happens to them?"

A line of muscle ticks in his jaw as he grinds his teeth together. "We don't know for certain. We only know they are here one minute, caught in between the next."

I swallow—the butterflies in my stomach once again making their overwhelming appearance.

"Alright, ladies first." He gestures his hand toward the tree.

"First? We can't go together?" I can't help the shake that overpowers my voice.

This is too much at one time. I wasn't prepared.

"The Janus Tree allows only one traveler at a time. This way, should someone be able to hide their intentions, a Kingdom will not be able to bring an entire army through at a moment's notice."

I nod, making note of that. It makes sense, but this is a tree we are talking about. None of it makes sense.

Clutching my bag of belongings tight, I grab hold of the smooth wooden handle in the center of the door. It's cool and firm to the touch, yet inviting and smooth under my fingertips. Wrenching the door open, I'm met with the sweet smell of smoke after a bonfire. All I can see is darkness between the amber glow radiating from nothingness.

"All you must do is walk forward. It will feel as if you blinked," Kori instructs, waiting behind me.

Steeling my nerves, I take a step forward and am met with shadows.

▲▲▲

I stumble through and find the other side's door wide open, only to realize I am no longer looking at the sunny, sand-filled hills of Paralia, but at the cloudy, majestic snow-capped mountains of Oresteia.

Immediately, a shiver runs through me as I adjust to the change in temperature.

Kori was not kidding when he said I needed a coat.

The sweat that had crusted my brow now cools to an unforgiving temperature. My long sleeves are doing nothing to curb the chill, considering this dress is made for an unrelenting sun.

As I try to move out of the doorway, I trip on a root peeking out of the snow-covered ground.

I drop my bag, arms flailing, hoping to catch myself before I end up both cold and wet.

All of a sudden, there are hands at my waist. Warmth seeps through my fabric as a stranger catches my fall and rights my stance. Taking my chin in their hand, they tilt my face up until our gazes meet.

The man looks into my eyes with an intensity that surpasses the chill I feel down to my bones.

And I find myself looking into a pair of familiar blue eyes.

He smiles at me, still holding lightly to my chin with one gloved hand, the other firm around my waist.

"Welcome to Oresteia."

CHAPTER SIX

Flustered, I blush and release myself from his grasp. With his hands leaving me, I'm met with the cold touch of the mountain air, and my skin mourns his contact.

I carefully begin walking backward just as Kori steps out of the Janus Tree. As he exits, the door disappears, leaving a bare trunk in its stead.

I cannot believe that just happened.

Kori makes eye contact with the man in front of me, nodding his head. "William," he cocks an eyebrow in annoyance. "I told you to stay back while I was away."

William smiles, reaching for my bag still lying in the snow. "I assumed our guest would not have the proper attire required for traveling such distances here in Oresteia, so I took it upon myself to bring more fitting wear."

I take my bag from his grasp and look down at my clothes compared to theirs. Worshiping the sun comes with a commitment to warmth and color. I own shades upon shades of dresses made of a light and breathable material. My closet is filled to the brim with lively hues.

William is wearing a fleece cloak over his tunic and trousers. His boots are leather, and his gloves are thick, but soft. I suppose I didn't notice it before when it was just King Kori before me, but they both wear exclusively white clothing with added gray detailing around the seams.

Nothing I packed is going to be wearable here. I'm not sure why I bothered.

Lifting my gaze, I study William's strong features. The people of Paralia are sun-soaked, and it shows on our skin, in our hair, and radiating from our eyes. Here, these two men look as though the mountain air has leached all the color from their features.

His pale skin contrasts mine, with hair so blonde it appears white. The only color found on him is the one in his gaze. Even then, that shade of blue is so icy I feel as though it might freeze me on the spot.

Kori clears his throat and moves around me to look down at William. "When I said stay, that was not a suggestion."

William just smiles and begins walking away. We are not in a hidden pocket in vines like we were in Paralia, but similarly, we are in a grove. These trees look similar to the peuko trees I've seen in books. Though, they were pictures I saw rather briefly.

As I follow William and Kori, I reach out to touch the sharp needles. The branches rustle softly in the breeze, their slender form brushing against my skin with a cutting feel.

Their long legs and snow-efficient boots travel much faster than I can. My flats are soaked, and my dress drags through the snow as I am left to lag while they murmur things to each other. Kori has placed a firm hand on William's shoulder as if to steer him in the direction of his choosing.

His knuckles look white, clasping firmly to him. My heart pains for William.

As we exit the small grove of peuko trees, William glances back over his shoulder at me. Excusing himself from King Kori, and prying himself from his grip, he pauses while I catch up to him. Needing a minute, I try to take a few deep breaths. The air is thinner here, and it tightens my chest.

"Please forgive me for not noticing before that you were carrying your bag." William takes the straps from me, heaving them over his left shoulder. In a moment, I feel as though I can breathe again. "My father should have been more courteous. I promise the rest of us in Oresteia are more hospitable." He winks at me, dawning a smile again.

"Your… father? Oh."

Of course he's the prince. He is the spitting image of the man who walked into our dining room yesterday. "I'm sorry, I hadn't realized I was walking with the prince." I attempt to curtsy, but he stops me with a light hand on my arm.

"None of that. You and I are of the same rank, the same age." He assesses me, top to bottom. "Your shoes and the bottom of your skirt are soaked through, and you must be freezing."

"I'm… attempting to get acclimated."

He laughs as I aim to make things feel casual between us while we walk. I am left out of breath at the exhilaration found in the sound of his laughter. Unlike his father, his smile appears to surface quite easily.

How refreshing.

"I brought items for you to put on that are more crafted for Oresteia weather than what you currently have, but you would not have been able to change at the Tree. We are almost to our first destination, though, and you may change there if you'd like."

"Oh, I hardly feel the chill at all now that my limbs are frozen solid." I hold up my hands to show the tint of blue they are beginning to reveal, assuming the rest of my body is looking the same.

He stops in his tracks.

"Penelope, forgive me. Years spent in a majority of solitude have wiped my mind blank. It's not often I am allowed to be in the company of someone I can offer help to. Here," he whips off his fleece cloak from around his neck to lay it across my shoulders. One by one, his gloves are peeled off and presented to me. "I'm used to the chill by now."

As soon as the gloves are on my hands and the cloak around my shoulders, I feel overwhelmingly more comfortable. The fleece has captured his body heat and is warming me from the inside out. Taking a deep breath, I'm met with the scent of cinnamon and vanilla.

"This cloak smells like a bakery!" I sigh, feeling more snug by the minute. It dawns on me that he used my name earlier, without me introducing myself. "I apologize if I'm missing something, but you know my name."

Sheepishly, he ducks his head as we continue forward. "I have… known… for a while that it would be you coming to Oresteia. I'm sorry if that caught you off guard."

I frown. "How long have you known? I only found out yesterday."

He seems to tiptoe around my question before answering. "Two months."

"Two months? When did your item go missing? Why was I not retrieved weeks ago?"

"There is much to tell you, but not much I can say. Once we get to the stronghold, and my father gives permission," he nods to Kori's back in front of us, "I will happily answer all the questions you can think of concerning why you are here. In the meantime, please ask me anything else, and I will oblige to your curiosities as I may."

I huff, rolling my eyes.

It's no matter, I am used to being left in the dark. I will read between the lines until I can receive more information.

"Where are we going? You said earlier we were headed to our 'first destination'."

"We should be arriving shortly. Oresteia is similar to Paralia in the way that we have a palace, and a city, with land in between. Though, here, our palace is our 'stronghold'." He quotes his last word with his fingers.

"Because the mountains make travel difficult, and snow a hefty burden, we cannot easily travel to all these places by foot. Our first stop is to the outskirt stables, where I acquired two horses and clothing for you for the ride."

He chuckles and shakes his head before continuing. "Had I not come, you would be sharing a cold ride with my father on the same horse in the same clothes you came with. I figured he would not think that far ahead, as he was primarily focused on getting in and out of Paralia."

I gasp, having focused only on his previous statement. "There are horses in Oresteia?"

His eyes liven as he says, "Wild horses are native to our mountain ranges. So many that we cannot keep up with them. The horses we have tamed for our army and personal use, like traveling, are but an inconsequential amount to what is running free in the rest of Oresteia."

My heartbeat quickens.

"Here, allow me to help you down this slope. If you look closely through the fog, you can see the outline of the stables just past the line of peuko trees at the bottom." He reaches out his bare hand, taking my gloved one in his. Hitching up my soaked skirt, we take small steps down the slope of this hill. I nearly pull him down with me at one point, but he swiftly catches my fall as he did when I tripped.

We reach the bottom of the hill, and William makes eye contact with me as he releases my hand. Again, I find my cheeks blushing. His eyes are alluring, drawing me into their icy depths.

▲▲▲

As we break the line of trees, a gravel path appears before us leading to a small gray, wooden stable. Smoke exits from the chimney on the roof, and I'm met with the smell of fresh hay in the air.

I'm so excited for a chance to warm up before heading to our next destination that my feet quicken on their own before I can even think about it.

We enter the small space and find Kori in a sitting room, one leg crossed over the other. Leaning back, he cocks an eyebrow at my bag that his son has been carrying, and the cloak and gloves that do not belong to me adorning my body.

"A snowstorm is on the horizon. We need to get moving. We wouldn't want our guest to get lost." Kori smirks at me.

Before I can respond, William moves in front of me to grab a small leather knapsack hanging on the wall next to the door we entered from. He hands it to me and looks toward his father. "There is always a snowstorm on the horizon. She has time to change." With his head, he gestures toward a small washroom tucked in the corner.

With the washroom door closed behind me, I make work of stripping out of my wet dress and flats quickly. Leaving those in the corner, I investigate the knapsack. It truthfully has everything I would need here—fleece trousers, a hefty tunic, a cloak just like William's, leather boots, and thick socks and gloves.

As I put the items on, I'm grateful for the extra warmth, but I mourn the colors of Paralia that typically grace my body.

Though, the white clothing does make the tan of my skin look enchanting.

On the wall, there's a small reflective glass hanging in front of me. My cheeks are red from the cold, and my bun has lost its shape from the wind. I do my best to smooth it down, but how it looks appears to be as good as it's going to get.

Walking back into the sitting room with the knapsack and William's cloak and gloves in hand, William's eyes land on mine as soon as I step back inside. He assesses me with his gaze, softly smiling with the corner of his mouth. In an attempt to avoid blushing again, I look around and find that Kori is nowhere to be found.

"Where did…"

"You look…" We speak at the same time, overlapping our words with one another. He gestures with his hand that I should speak first, miming that his mouth is locked shut.

"Where did King Kori go?" I ask. "Unfortunately, my father can be quite impatient. He doesn't enjoy being outside of our stronghold for too long, lest something happen when he's away. He has already begun the journey back."

I nod, understanding that. My father is the same way.

William looks at me questioningly, as if asking whether or not it's his turn to speak. I smile, moving forward to act as if I'm taking a key to his lips to unlock his mouth.

"You look radiant in Oresteia white." He blurts, as if he could not contain that sentence for another second.

I blush again and divert my eyes from his.

What about this stranger has made me easily become so comfortable in his presence already?

"Thank you," I whisper. "I hope it's okay, but I left my previous clothing in the washroom. I don't think I'll be needing it here."

"That is perfectly fine. I'll have someone come up in a few days to retrieve it." He moves to take the items from my hands, placing his gloves back on, and flinging the cloak and knapsack behind his shoulder.

"I've never ridden a horse before, so I'm not sure how much help I'll be…" I trail off, following him down a hall toward the smell of hay.

We enter the stall part of the stable and William responds, "I had assumed you might not have ridden before. We will be sharing my horse, and you won't need to do anything at all."

He gestures toward the end of the stalls, where a black horse leans its head out of the top part of the stall door. Huffing at William, it begins to stomp its hooves on the ground, tossing its head up and down.

William laughs, bringing a hand to its nose. "Penelope, this is my most trusted friend, Agrius. I caught and broke him myself, but he will never be fully tamed like any of our others. It's how he got his name."

Smiling from ear to ear, I bring my hand up to pet Agrius on the nose. He nudges my fingers, allowing me to lay my palm on his muzzle. As I pet him, I ask, "What do you mean how he got his name?"

"His name means *wild*. I've come across many horses, and many other animals in the mountains of

Oresteia, but I have never met a wilder beast than Agrius."

Breaking my petting trance, William says, "Are you ready to go? I brought him here not long before you and my father showed up, so he's ready for the trip back."

Hesitantly, I nod. I'm not sure what to expect, but how bad could it be?

CHAPTER SEVEN

Apparently, very bad.

William helps me onto Agrius, allowing my foot to step onto his interlocked fingers. After taking three tries to swing my leg across like he showed me first, he eventually leaves to find a small footstool hidden in the attic of the stables for me to use.

Once I'm firmly on, William swings up behind me with ease. He attaches my bag and the knapsack securely behind us, and we are finally on our way.

Even though I am sitting in front of William with his arms locking me into place, I can hardly stay in my seat. The wind whistles past my ears as we ride, faster than I thought horses could run. Snow begins falling soon into the journey, and I cannot hear or see anything.

The rhythmic motion of the horse beneath me is exhilarating. My fingers tremble slightly as I reach out to stroke Agrius' neck, feeling the warmth of his muscular frame beneath his glossy coat. The scent of hay and leather mingle with one of vanilla and cinnamon.

I shiver under the cold air's touch, and William laughs behind me.

Shouting, he leans in as he says, "You'll get used to it!"

I shake my head, knowing if I tried to shout back, the wind would easily steal my voice from his ears. Besides, I don't know how to explain to him that I do not yet miss the sun's embrace; that I've yearned for climate change for years.

As the night sky begins to show, the snowfall slows, and so do we. I have no idea where we've come from, or where we are going. Surveying my surroundings, I notice that everything from the ground beneath Agrius' feet to the mountains looming in the distance is covered in thick, white frost.

"Are we going to make it before nightfall?" I ask, turning around as much as I'm able so he can better hear me.

"Look ahead—do you see those lights beginning to turn on in that mountain valley?" He points in the direction we are heading.

"They look like stars!" I gasp, squinting toward the lights.

He laughs, putting his arm back down around me to grasp Agrius' mane. "That's Copolis—our city. The name roughly translates to mean 'snow valley'." He laughs again, the sound echoing off behind me. "Unfortunately, it's very rare for them to see anything but snow on the ground. Occasionally, on our warmer days, it will pack down into ice, but very rarely do we get to see the yellow grass beneath."

I look around as we move past, noticing how built into the mountainscape the buildings are now that more and more lights are coming on.

"Where is your stronghold? Are we still far from it?" My head is still turned to better amplify my voice in his direction, and I see a smile creep up into his face.

"If we continue, past the city, there's a mountain range closing in Copolis on the far side. Do you see that?" I nod. "That mountain is *Escaeus*, meaning 'hidden strength'. There, at the base, there is a gate known only to Oresteians. Our stronghold is within."

Appalled, I ask, "*In* the mountain? How did it get there? How does that work?"

Smiling at me again, he says, "You'll see."

▲▲▲

As we move past Copolis, William tells me that at this time of night, the city is usually full of life.

"Because we are on the verge of having a bigger-than-normal snowstorm tonight, many of them closed their shops early to lock up their doors and windows. Whereas in Paralia you worship the sun, here, we worship the stars." He glances up into the night sky, watching the stars slowly become covered by clouds moving in from the East.

I lean my head back, resting it gently on his shoulder—taking in the sky as dusk envelopes us in peaceful darkness. "It's so quiet," I whisper, to not disturb the silence. I can feel his chest rise and fall behind me, and I begin mimicking his deep breaths.

Closing my eyes briefly, I allow the mountain air to fill my lungs. I feel Agrius strong beneath me, and William steady behind me. The buzz of bugs coming to life around us echoes in my ears. The cool winter air frosts my nose. My breathing slows, and I allow rest to overcome my senses.

▲▲▲

I'm shoved awake by an elbow in my side. William whispers, "You might want to be awake for this."

Wearily willing my eyelids to open, we have made it to what I'm assuming is the entrance to the stronghold. The mountain looms above me, and I crane my neck to look at its peak. Agrius slows, walking to a stop as we come to stand before a black iron gate cut into the mountain's side. The shadows are colder than the air outside—if that's even possible.

Two men blend into the shadows next to the gate, dressed in black. Swords strapped down their backs, they come to stand in front of us.

"Our gatekeepers," William points out to me.

"Men, I've traveled far and wide and seek entry. The point has come to pass." His voice takes an authoritative tone when speaking to them, echoing off the mountain walls.

The gatekeepers respond while backing up, one on each side of us. "The stars will lead the way." At the same time, they each lay their hand on the rock walls, and the iron gate begins to open. Agrius starts moving forward without any prompt from William, seemingly used to this pattern.

I feel William nod to the two men behind me, but I keep my eyes low and forward. I map out where their hands were placed, and how long the gate stays open once their hands are removed.

Thirty seconds.

The tunnel we enter is lit by lamps along the side, coaxing us deeper into the mountain. Trying to break the silence, I ask, "Why were the gatekeepers in black, rather than the white I've seen you and your father wear?"

"White is only for the royal family. It exudes purity, riches, and honor. Should we be hit in battle, those around us would immediately know where and how badly by the blood that shows through. Should we need to travel a distance without someone tracking us, white helps us blend into our surroundings.

"Black uniforms for our guards and watchers keep them hidden in the shadows. In this case, under Escaeus, a traveler could come across this entrance. Our gatekeepers are under strict order to stay back unless someone directly approaches. The wording I used was in code, and those who live in the stronghold would tell you they'd rather die than let those words be carved from their tongue."

William's posture straightens as he speaks, becoming more 'prince' by the minute.

We turn the corner, and suddenly the tunnel opens into a wide cavern littered with glowing green lights. Stretching as tall as Escaeus itself, built into the side of the mountain, is the stronghold. Flowing out of the mountain wall, a stream runs next to us, roaring amid silence.

I gasp in astonishment at the size of this place. "Was this… carved out of Escaeus?"

"Rock by rock, column by column, window by window, our stronghold was carved out by the earliest Oresteians. It was either this, or on top of Escaeus, and they decided that to hide inside the mountain was to trust the land to hold us firm. In a way, it keeps us humble, knowing our safe place could fall on us at any time. We are at the mercy of Oresteia."

"I often feel that way in regard to Paralia's palace. With our unpredictable high tides, we can only pray to the sun that the columns beneath us will stand fast against the current."

Crossing over a wooden bridge, a tall iron door slams open in front of us, and King Kori stalks out, meeting us where we are.

"You're late," he snaps, crossing his arms over his chest.

"We must have lost track of time—Penelope was enjoying the view." William jumps off Agrius with ease, lending me a hand once he's firmly footed on the rocky path.

Slowly, I ease off the horse's tall back, fixing my cloak once I'm down. I try to curtsy to Kori, but my legs are stiff, and my back aches.

Kori waves me off, giving William a pointed glare. "Take Agrius to his stable and meet me inside at once. You've kept us waiting."

Grabbing my bag and the knapsack from the back

of Agrius, he says, "I need to show Penelope to her room, and then I can meet you wherever you wish."

"That is unnecessary. I've already asked Selene to take care of Penelope's needs this evening. Because you decided to leave today against my wishes, we are behind."

William laughs and shakes his head.

I look at him, asking, "Selene?"

He smiles at me. "Selene."

CHAPTER EIGHT

WILLIAM LEAVES WITH AGRIUS, AND I FOLLOW KORI inside the stronghold.

Kori snaps his fingers as we enter, and immediately a girl about my age comes sauntering out of the hall nearby, emitting assurance. As she approaches, my eyes roam around the room. The entrance is vast; the ceilings reach up to as high as the mountain itself. There are two staircases on either side, winding up toward lofts upon lofts railed with balcony edges.

"Selene, Penelope. Penelope, Selene." Kori waves between the girl—Selene—and myself, turning to walk toward the left staircase. Without another word, and not a glance backward, Kori disappears, and it is just me and her.

Once Kori is gone, Selene's pale face brightens into a smile. Her dark hair contrasts her skin tone, making her dark eyes pop as they look me over from head to toe.

"Penelope! I have heard so much about you." She

squeezes me tight like one would an old friend. Sheepishly, I smile back, unsure how to tell her I have no idea who she is. "I'm here to take you to your room. Let me grab that from you." She takes the small knapsack, slinging it across her shoulder.

"I feel like I have been waiting ages for you to get here. I'm sure the journey felt just as long to you, if not longer." She raises an eyebrow at me, questioning, "Have you ever ridden horseback before?"

"No, we don't have horses in Paralia. Agrius was an unexpected treat." I answer, hoping my stiff legs do not hinder me from following her wherever we are headed.

Selene nods, then begins to walk toward one of the staircases. "William is sure to be kicking himself for not getting to be the one to take you to where you'll be staying. I told him that leaving to meet you and Kori would be a terrible idea, but he's not often persuaded by the wisdom I offer." She shrugs, her hair flinging over her shoulder with the move.

Rather than taking the stairs—thank the sun—we turn into a doorway underneath the staircase. Laying her palm on the doorknob, it gives off a slight orange glow before swinging open. Looking forward, silver-plated wooden doors are lining each side from where we stand to where the hall ends.

"This is the family's quarters. There is no need for there to be *this* many rooms, but I suppose they were hoping Oresteians would breed like rabbits." She laughs, looking at me over her shoulder. "I hear you have six siblings?"

Taken aback at the slight insult, I nod.

"I don't know how you do it. William and I are both only children. I wouldn't want it any other way."

We reach the end of the hall, and she gestures to the room on the far right.

"This one is yours. I'm across the hall." She points. "And William is in the one to your right. Kori is the first door to your left when you enter the hallway. The door to enter and leave the hall is enchanted, much like the Janus Tree. Having the blood of a royal should allow you to come and go as you please. If you have issues, let us know."

Her eyes connect with the bag I've been carrying. "You didn't pack much—not that Paralian clothing will do too much for you here. I'm sure they arranged for items to be put in your room for you, but if not, you can always borrow something of mine for the time being."

I look over her outfit, dark red from shoulders to shoes. Her clothes don't look quite as thick and warm as mine are, but perhaps that is because they are not fit for travel. She's still wearing boots like the rest of us, but they are shorter at the ankle and have a slight heel to them that clack as she walks on the tile floors.

"Dinner is in half an hour, but I can get it brought to you if you need a minute to breathe."

"That would be perfect, thank you. Are the bedroom doors enchanted as well?" I ask, unsure of how all this works.

Oresteia feels like a whole new planet compared to Paralia.

"Only yourself, and those you allow entry, will be able to get in. We value privacy here. Don't feel as though just because someone may ask you to open the door, or let them in, you have to. Behind that door is *your* safe space."

She cocks her head as she smiles at me. "Of course, I'm talking about myself. Once we know each other better, I will beg to be allowed inside your room. I've never had another female my age living in the stronghold, and because of that, I have no boundaries."

I smile back at her, warming up to her upfront spirit. "How did you come to live in the stronghold on this floor? One must assume you are also royalty, though you are not wearing Oresteia white?"

She claps her hands together, squealing in delight. "I'm William's cousin! His mom and my mom were sisters. I cannot believe he didn't tell you before you arrived." She places a hand in her trouser pocket, exuding confidence with her stance. "I don't wear white because they wear white. Black was, unfortunately, out of the question due to me not being part of the guard. Red was the next best color."

"Do other colors not exist in Oresteia?" I ask.

"Not as they do in Paralia. Because of the mountain's unrelenting temperatures, we require specific types of clothing to not freeze to death. Structuring our clothes with fur, fleecing lining, and heavy material requires a lot of time and effort. Adding a dye to the material makes that process take much longer.

"Tromping around in the snow and ice wears our clothes down faster, so we go through things like that." She snaps her fingers. "I do not often go *trekking* through the elements, so I'm allowed a few red outfits if I promise I will make them 'last'." She quotes, huffing into the air.

I nod in understanding. I do not feel as though I'll be able to wear my current white outfit again for a few days, as the falling snow soaked through much of the top layer. Thinking of the temperature from outside makes me shiver, remembering just how cold I was on the journey here.

Selene notes my chill and gestures back toward my bedroom door. "Now that I've talked your ear off, I'll leave you to it. I'll make sure dinner is brought to you within the hour." She tugs on the knapsack on her shoulder, securing it again, and turns on her heel to walk back toward where we came.

Left alone, I place my hand on my bedroom door.

The knob glows, and the door swings wide open, beckoning me inside.

CHAPTER NINE

The first thing I notice are the windows.

Wide-eyed, I drop my bag and slowly spin in a circle as I survey my new home.

On my left, tall windows overtake the wall, displaying the snowstorm that is beginning to brew over the horizon. Heavy grey curtains drape on either side of the glass panes, begging to be pulled closed to create a cocoon of darkness.

I run my hand over the fleece-lined material, relishing in just how soft the fabric of the curtains are. Along the left wall, there's a small marble white desk sitting in the corner. Upon further inspection, the drawers are empty, save for a black vase sitting empty on top.

I return to my bag sitting on the warm stone floor and retrieve the journal and dagger I brought from Paralia. After placing those in the top right drawer of the desk, I realize I forgot to bring a writing utensil with me.

I will have to ask Selene later where I can get one, so I might write Callious at once.

Tucked away in the wall opposite the door, there's an open-shelved closet, filled with clothing items for various events. Cloaks, trousers, and tunics like I am wearing now, but also dresses, skirts, and a few softer, loose-fitting sets made for sleeping. Everything is colored in shades of white—ranging from snow-colored to cream. Detailing is lined in gray, silver, or black.

I drag my bag to the closet, unable to find the strength to lift and carry it. I begin unpacking the few clothing items I was able to bring: my flats, three dresses ranging from blue to green in various shades, and a few hair accessories. Absent-mindedly, I find myself reaching up to touch the necklace Callious made for me.

Sighing, I collapse in an exhausted heap on the closet floor.

I've only just arrived, and I already feel as though I do not belong. This world is a stranger to me, and I am a stranger to it.

Emptying my bag, the only thing left to unpack is my blanket throw from Paralia. Mother made every Frey a blanket when they were born, depicting with color who she and father hoped they would be when they grew up.

Pulling it over my body, I huddle into its familiar warmth. My throw is hand-knit with the softest yarn I have ever felt. The color of the rising sun, my parents hoped their youngest, and last, daughter would bring new beginnings to Paralia.

I'm not quite sure this is what they envisioned.

Standing, I tuck my bag away in the closet and find the bed.

Much like the curtains, the quilt is fleece- lined and dark gray in color. Bigger than anything I had in Paralia, I feel as though I could fit four people within the covers. There is a small nightstand in between the closet and the bed, holding an oil lamp and another empty black vase.

Laying my blanket over the quilt, the room immediately brightens. Smiling to myself, I run my hand over the bed as I move toward the corner opposite the closet, where the washroom is beckoning.

Just like the closet, there is no door to separate this space from the rest of the room. Walking through the entryway, a bathtub made of marble stone and silver furnishings takes up most of the space, calling my name. A wooden tray lays across the tub walls, holding an unlit candle and bars of soap.

Next to the bath, there is a mirror my size leaning against the adjacent wall. Surveying my face and hair, I cringe as I see myself for the first time since the outskirt stable.

Turning on the bathtub's tap, hot water runs out of the faucet. Grinning from ear to ear, I go back into the closet to grab a pants and shirt set I can wear to bed. The flowy, white fabric is soft between my fingers.

If Selene is meaning to bring me dinner soon, I don't have much time. Hopefully, that means I can have the evening to myself.

Removing my riding gear, I dip into the hot water and lean my head back, allowing my curly hair to release from the bun it's been in. Massaging my fingers through my hair, I release the tension I've felt in my scalp all day.

The soap on the tray smells like the peuko trees we passed—full of earth and pine. I lather the soap over my body, wiping off the grime and cold from my skin.

Dunking myself under the warm water once more, I allow myself a moment of solitude under the surface. If I close my eyes, I can pretend I'm simply basking under the Neronian Sea, waiting for the sun to set.

I heave myself out of the tub, dripping water all over the stone floor before wrapping a soft, white towel around my body. Using another to dry my hair, I walk to the small stool next to the mirror where I set my new clothes.

Already, my skin has brightened. My hair will have to air dry as I sleep, but it is soft and knot-free.

Dawning on the sleep set, I begin to brush out my curls with my fingers. Satisfied, I lay my towels out over the tub walls and pad back into my bedroom.

Next to the bed, I find a pair of white slippers tucked away under the overhang of the quilt. Sitting on the edge of the bed, I slip them on and wiggle my feet in the furred interior.

I lay back on the mattress, spreading my arms out. Tiredness hits me out of nowhere, reminding me just how much I've done today. I debate forsaking dinner to go straight to sleep, but I have not eaten a single thing since yesterday's evening meal.

I wonder what Callious is doing.

A knock at my door causes me to shoot straight up, and my empty stomach growls in protest. Walking over,

I whisk the door open expecting to see Selene, only to be face-to-face with William once more.

He grins at me, taking in the Oresteian outfit I'm wearing. "I heard you needed dinner."

I step back, saying, "I had presumed it would be Selene bringing it. Does King Kori no longer need your assistance?"

William presents a platter of food to me from where he had been hiding it behind his back. "You will find, Penelope Frey, that my father does not truly need me for many things."

The scent of it all hits my nose, and I find myself involuntarily salivating over the smell. Some kind of meat, potatoes, vegetables, and bread layered in butter cover every inch of the plate he holds.

William laughs as he witnesses my eye contact become glued to the stash in his hands. Handing the plate over to me, he says, "If you have any preference on what you are served, feel free to let me know so I can alert the kitchen. Hopefully this will suffice for tonight."

Barely able to contain my delight, I exclaim, "This is *perfect*. Thank you!"

"If there's nothing else you'll be needing, I'll be retiring for the night as well." He points to the door to the right of mine. "That is my door—you are welcome to knock at any time." He smiles at me again, bowing his head. "Goodnight, Penelope."

"Goodnight," I call, shutting my door with my foot and walking the plate carefully to my desk. As I set my dinner down, I remember my journal tucked away in the drawer.

I forgot to ask for a pen.

CHAPTER TEN

I WAKE UP IN THE MORNING TO BRIGHT LIGHT reflecting off the piles of snow outside my windows. Even though the sky is overcast and foggy, the snow shines vibrantly into my eyes with the daytime glow.

Stretching, I reorient my senses to remind myself where I am. The bed is soft below me, beckoning me to answer to its restful call again.

Unsure of what time it is, I heave myself out of the comfort of my quilt and move toward the windows.

How do they tell time here without being able to see the sun?

I pull my curtains open, hoping to catch a glimpse of someone walking around. Instead, I am met with mountain range after mountain range looming in front of my eyes. Snow cascades down the summit as the fog and clouds wrap around the base.

The snow on the ground has drifted against my windows, piling up to be half my height. If I look closely, the blanket of white covering the ground glitters. Untouched, the mound of snow looks crisp and welcoming.

The wind catches the top layer of snow, swirling it around the window like a bird catching a breeze. I lean in to place my hands on the cold glass, and my breath fogs the window, leaving condensation in its wake. Running my finger through the vapor left on the surface, I write '*PENELOPE*' in capital letters.

In the hall, a door slams, startling me out of my dreamlike state. I allow myself one last glance at the weather outside, then rush to get ready for the day.

I don't want to miss a single thing.

▲▲▲

Once I've dressed in the warmest clothing I can find, I quietly move through the hall, wondering if Selene or William are awake. I debate knocking on Selene's door, but if it's later in the day, I don't want to risk embarrassing myself by not being up at an earlier hour.

My boots echo off the hallway tile, announcing my presence as I open the door to the foyer where I arrived just yesterday. There are large double doors to my right —presumably a great hall, or the dining room.

The stairs on either side of this foyer piqued my interest last night, watching them wind up the side of the stronghold. Moving toward the left-hand staircase, my eyes stretch up to the four lofted balconies above me, reaching to the ceiling.

Taking the first flight of stairs two steps at a time, I reach the first level and lay my hand along the silver balcony railing. Cool to the touch, the metal shines under my fingers. On the second floor, the mountain wall opens up to allow three doors to sit within it. The middlemost door is wide open, begging me to walk inside to see what it might hide.

As I enter, my eyes adjust to the darkness of the room. The cool stone interior reminds me that I am *inside* a mountain—carved out whole to be their stronghold.

Lamps line the wall unlit, except for one in the far-right corner of the room. The ceiling is vast, angled in a way that makes me think this room was not always here.

A melody floats along the space, meeting my ears with delight. As I walk deeper into the room, I find that past the lit lamp, there is a black curtain blocking off the rest of the room. Velvet to the touch, I pull it back gently. Behind it, I find the source of the music.

William, playing piano, sits behind the curtain near the wall adjacent to me. His white clothing in addition to the white gleam of the instrument shines brightly in this dark, cool room.

A vibrant song voices itself from his fingertips as he plays. Eyes closed, his head leans back as if he is resting in the sound of his music.

Occasionally, a smile graces his lips as chords progress, evoking emotion long tucked away. He leans forward slightly, as if drawn closer by the melody itself, held in anticipation of the next phrase.

I move behind the curtain again, careful to not be seen, as I stand and listen to what he has to play. Minutes pass, and my eyes close of their own volition, as if they cannot help but relish in the sound of his tune.

"You may move to listen closer if you'd like." William's voice pulls my head out of the clouds, jarring me. His hands continue to move along the keys as he looks over his shoulder at me, nodding his head toward the other side of the piano bench he sits on.

Looking back toward the door I came from, I debate whether to stay or leave. Not knowing where I would go from here, I move out from behind the curtain.

"What do you call that song?" I ask, moving to stand next to his bench.

"I call that 'A Summer Day'. Though, it's been a long time since I've experienced anything but ice and snow."

I smile. "I think you captured it perfectly. Better than I could ever do—I was never given the chance to take instrumental lessons."

"I taught myself. I found my mind wandering toward harmonies and melodies at a very early age, and father didn't know what to do with it. We carved out this space between two council rooms on this floor and it has been mine ever since."

"What is the curtain for? To hide the piano?" I run my hand along the sleek surface, marveling at the craftsmanship it took to create such a thing.

"The curtain is to create an illusion that this space is empty and vast. I prefer to play with the door open, but the curtain helps block the sound from escaping."

I shift to sit beside him on the bench, lightly

hovering my fingertips over the ivory keys. "How did you know I was listening?"

He smiles again, looking down. "I had hoped you'd find your way in here. I figured you may want to get to know your new home before you get thrown into everything else."

"And what, exactly, am I getting thrown into? All I've been told is that I'm here to help search for something that Oresteia believes Paralia stole."

William shuffles off the bench, placing the lid over the keys. Holding his hand out to me, he says, "I can give you answers, but not here."

Curiosity taking hold of me, I grasp his hand and allow him to lead me out of the room.

I glance back at the piano one last time, mourning its song.

CHAPTER ELEVEN

I follow William back to the staircase, and we begin winding up the remaining two floors.

"Are you hungry?" William asks as we reach the top.

Hardly out of breath due to the stairs I take so often from Paralia's shores, I respond, "Not at the moment. What time is it? I haven't seen anyone else so far today."

"It's just past dawn—around 6 in the morning."

Shocked, I look out the window to my right, hoping to find some sign that it is that early. "How can you tell so easily what time it is? In Paralia, we go by the sun's shadow."

William shrugs, holding open a door for me at the end of the loft's hall. "You will grow used to the fact that our days look the same. Your internal clock will begin to just know."

"You believe I will be here long enough for that to take place?"

He nods, allowing me to pass by him. As our gazes collide, I make note of a small scar under his left eye. Turned upward, it blends in with the lines brought by his smile.

Moving into the dark space, William closes the door behind me and a fire in the middle of the room immediately roars to life. Illuminated by the flames, shelves upon shelves of books jump out in front of my eyes, building a library more extensive than one I've ever seen.

I gasp, and William laughs behind me.

The stone fireplace reaches to the ceiling, appearing as if it was cut from the mountain itself. A black leather couch sits by the fire, glistening in the flame's light. A dark wooden table and chairs stand in the middle of it all.

Books line the walls to my right and my left, stretching as high as I can see. A rolling ladder attaches itself to the wall on either side, begging to be climbed upon and pushed.

Distracted by the beauty, I fail to notice William has already moved on to sit by the fire, leaning back in one of the wooden chairs. A rolled- up piece of parchment materializes on the table in front of him as he places a hand on top.

Shaking myself from my daze, I move to claim one of the other chairs, keeping my eyes on the paper.

"How are you doing that?" I ask, lowering myself into the seat.

William takes hold of the scroll and looks up at me. A reflection of flames burns in his eyes, making his blue irises feel warmer and colder all at the same time. The seriousness in his gaze freezes me to my seat.

"What do you know of Oresteia, Penelope?" He asks, leaning forward to rest his elbows on the table. Hands clasped together holding the paper, his tone lowers as his gaze drops to look up at me through his brows.

Sheepishly, I look down to my lap, playing with the pockets of my trousers. "I was not… permitted… to be part of many discussions. There would be no chance that I would need any information delivered in those meetings, so I was told to bide my time in other ways."

I still my hands, sighing. Looking back up at William, I see understanding in his eyes. "I suppose that's my long way of saying I do not know much, but I am more than willing to learn."

William grins, slapping the scroll against his knee. "*That* is what I was hoping to hear. Many outside of Oresteia have… opinions about what they believe goes on within our cavern walls. Your current lack of knowledge is not something to be ashamed of—it is a victory.

"Very few individuals allow themselves to open their mind long enough for an Oresteian to speak our truth into it. Because of that, our ways often get warped into a watered-down version of who we are."

My heart quickens, feeling honored that I get to sit and hear what a first-hand account of their history might be. "If you'll allow me to know, I am willing to listen."

His smile broadens. "Then let's begin."

▲▲▲

William quickly calls for food to be brought up to us, stating that we might be here awhile.

Soon enough, a silver platter layered with a spread of eggs, biscuits, jam, bacon, and oatmeal is laid on the table.

My stomach growls as the smell wafts to encompass the space. We dig in—a comfortable silence filling in the gaps between us. The parchment has long since been placed before William again, with the accompaniment of a few books pulled from the shelves around us.

Though I've only known William for a day, I find myself at ease around him in a way I only have been with Callious. There's something familiar about his easy-going demeanor. Whereas his father's aura came across as a bitter cold wind and harsh lines, William's is softer, calmer. If he were Paralian, I would liken him to a gentle afternoon summer breeze drifting through my hair.

"What are you pondering?" William asks in between bites of breakfast.

"What makes you think I'm pondering about anything?"

"Your dark eyes lit up." He smiles, pointing at my fork. "And you stopped eating mid-bite."

I laugh, lifting my food to my mouth and wave the fork around. "Maybe I'm not hungry anymore." I finish the bite, winking at him as I place my hands next to my plate.

"The only meal you've had in nearly two days is

what I brought to you last night. I hardly doubt that has been enough to sustain you from what these days have held."

Rolling my eyes, I wipe my hands on the napkin in my lap and place it over my empty plate. Finishing his food, William leans back in his chair and rolls up his sleeves.

Clearing his throat, he says, "It would be a disservice to you for me to only tell you what I know of Oresteia. Rather, I must *show* you for things to make sense." He pauses, cocking his head to the left. "Selene, you can come out now."

Out from the shadows of the bookshelves, Selene saunters out, smiling at me. She waves, moving to tuck a piece of hair behind her ear. Now standing at William's right, she excitedly bounces from foot to foot.

"Penelope," William says, regaining my focus. "Welcome, again, to Oresteia." He nods at Selene, and she brings her hand out in front of her body.

Her fingertips catch fire, flame burning from the ends of her hand.

Gasping, I lean back in my chair to avoid the sudden heat. My eyes widen out of their sockets as she brings her other hand forward to bounce the fire back and forth between her two palms.

As quickly as they caught fire, her fingertips extinguish as if there was never a flame in the first place. She waves a hand toward the fireplace, and the roaring logs are put out in an instant. Waving her hand again, the fire catches once more.

She snaps her fingers, and the lamps around the room suddenly light at once, banishing the shadows from the shelves. Again, with a snap, the lights are off just as they were before.

Selene places her hands back in front of her, clasping them as if they were not engulfed in flames just mere minutes ago.

I look between her and William, waiting for an explanation of what I just saw.

"You have… magic?" I ask, my voice small and full of wonder.

They smile as William leans forward onto the table. "Oresteia *is* magic."

CHAPTER TWELVE

William thanks Selene for the demonstration, sending her on her way. Grabbing the parchment, he unrolls it and places it flat in front of him and me. Depicted on the paper is a drawing of a crown.

Wrapped in silver, the crown's metal twists around itself like a vine. In the middle, three black stones are set on either side of a bigger, lighter- colored gem. The white sparkle of the middle jewel is clear, setting it apart from the others. As I trace my finger over the detailing, William begins:

"This is the Oresteian Queen's Crown. Crafted by rulers before us, it has been passed down from genera- tion to generation. This crown is not to be worn, but to behold. Set on a white pillow made of velvet in a casing made of the clearest of glasses, it sits next to the thrones of the Oresteian royal family.

"The crown is guarded at all times. The casing is enchanted so only one with the blood of a royal may open it. Even then, there has never been a reason for the crown to be touched or taken. It is our most sacred artifact—one we hold most dear."

William sighs, raking a hand through his thick hair. "The jewel in the middle is known as the Queen's Heart. Found long ago, it allows the royal family to manipulate Oresteia's magic in specific ways. Selene can control small amounts of light or flame and wield them to her advantage. My father and I have more…" he hesitates, "concentrated uses of magic."

"And your mother? The queen?"

He smiles softly at me, his eyes growing sad. "We have no queen; I have no mother. She succumbed to the stars when I was around nine years of age."

I reach out to touch his hand, allowing my sorrow to be conveyed without words.

"My mother could speak to the stars—hear their wishes. In the end, it drove her mad to know so much, but be able to do so little. Her health degenerated with her mind." He pulls his hand from mine, pointing to the jewel in the middle.

"This is why you are here, Penelope. The Queen's Heart was stolen—replaced with a fake—three months previous. Father believes it was Paralia to have taken it, though many others are not convinced—myself included."

He pauses. "We have searched high and low to no end. Father believes that by using you as a bargaining chip, the Frey will give it back to us, lest war be proclaimed."

"I can assure you; I have no part in this. I have not seen this jewel previous to this encounter. As I've said before, I was not allowed to be part of many things. Your father would have been better off calling for one of my siblings," I say, exasperated.

William leans back in his chair. "That's the thing— I believe father brought you because he knew that. I hold to the belief that my father *wants* to go to war with Paralia. What he has to gain, I have no idea. Maybe it's pride. But you, Penelope, can help me avoid that from happening."

I ponder his words, musing it all over.

It is a completely different world here.

And yet, it feels… natural.

"How is Selene still able to wield her magic with the jewel missing? I would assume the same to be true regarding you and your father."

"The Queen's Heart funnels its gift into Oresteia's land from where it sits on the crown. Built upon a foundation of magic, our stronghold within Escaeus holds the magic in reserves. It's what allows me to do things like make this parchment appear out of thin air, or light the fireplace when I walk into a room.

"With the Queen's Heart sitting in its rightful place, we can use our magic throughout all of Oresteia. Without it, we are bound to this stronghold. Eventually, the reserves will run dry, and our abilities with it."

"Coming from a land without magic, I don't personally see the direness of the situation. Your father is willing to send men to war if his 'special gem' is not found so he can… keep his magical powers?" I huff.

"I, too, had begun that train of thought. While I love what Oresteia gives, I do not think it warrants the deaths of many." Pulling out one of the books from his stack, it falls open on the table between us.

William flips to the middle, skimming each page before landing his finger on a picture. "What do you see here?"

I peek, trying to make sense of the drawing. "Is that the Janus Tree?"

He smiles. "It is. According to this, the Janus Tree also siphons from the Queen's Heart. When the bargain of peace was made between the King of Paralia and the King of Oresteia, the blood that flowed from their hands created the Janus Tree. The Queen's Heart was wedged inside the tree, found by the Oresteian King.

"The Queen's Heart exists because of the Janus Tree, and the Tree because of the Heart. They are interconnected."

Nervously, William closes the book once more. "This account goes on to say that should the Queen's Heart be missing from Oresteia for too long, the Janus Tree will cease to exist." He looks around the room, leaning in closer to me to whisper, "And should the Janus Tree cease to exist, so too will our lands."

I gasp, processing what he just said. After a stretch of silence, I say, "William, I would love to help, but I don't know the first place to start. I am deeply unqualified for something like this." I wring my hands in my lap, mind racing.

He leans forward to tuck a piece of hair behind my ear. "No one believes either of us has anything to offer. My father has asked me to stay out of it—to keep you busy. Your father did not allow you to learn the things you should have, being one of many royal heirs. Let us prove them wrong. Let us save our Kingdoms, Penelope."

My eyes wander, finding anywhere but his gaze to hold onto.

Finally making eye contact once more, I ask, "You say it's already been three months?" William nods. "Show me where to start."

He laughs, crossing his arms over his chest. "I thought you'd never ask."

▲▲▲

Many hours later, a kettle of coffee is placed before me. I pour some into a cup and take it into my hands, relishing the warmth it brings. As I pour a cup for William, I ask, "How do you like your coffee?"

He smirks as he answers, "With you."

I shake my head. "How can you make that judgment based on the so little knowledge you have regarding me?"

"You're right. We hardly know each other." He grabs my chair and pulls me to be next to him, spilling *my* coffee in the process. "Here is my thought—every time I see you, I will ask you a new question in the hope of getting to know you just a little bit better. Whatever the question, you must be truthful in your answer."

I scoff, shifting to place my coffee cup on the table. "That sounds like a subtle way to pry into my life at your jurisdiction."

"Penelope, you didn't let me finish. Once the question has left my lips, I will either answer the same question myself, or you can ask your own. Either way, I vow to be ever honest with how I respond."

My smile picks up at the chance to get to know him a bit better as well. All this talk of Oresteia has left me longing for more.

"Deal," I say, as I hold out my hand.

"Deal." We shake, our gazes locked. *What have I just gotten myself into?*

"I'll begin. What's your favorite color?" He asks, an eyebrow cocked.

I laugh. "That's your big question?"

"Time is ticking, Penelope. If you don't answer this question truthfully, you'll find that my next question is much more… personal."

I ponder his words. "Okay…" While I think, I look him over from head to toe.

What does he know of color?

"Green—like the Neronian Sea." I answer quickly. "What is *your* favorite color?"

"What color would you consider your eyes?" He says, peering into my very soul. Taken aback, I'm left without words.

"Brown isn't a very fascinating color in comparison to all your other options," I remark.

He leans back in his chair. "I would have to disagree. Your eyes are not just brown—they are the golden color of honey, the dark depths of a cup of coffee. They reflect the fire's light within them—captivating me with their flame. I would dare say brown is the only logical answer to that question."

My jaw drops, stunned.

No one has ever described such a trivial part of myself like that before.

"Quit showing off," I say, elbowing him in the side. He laughs, head tilted back in delight.

This will be fun.

CHAPTER THIRTEEN

Lunch was brought to us in the library—the afternoon coming and going. William and I spent hours poring over books, theories, and information. Being that all I had to offer is a listening ear, the conversations were very one-sided.

Just before evening broke, he was summoned by a guard to meet with the King. Taking that as my chance to collect my thoughts, I found a pen stowed away in one of the books and retired back to my room, intending to write Callious with everything I've learned thus far.

I know my father demanded I write to him, but I have yet to be able to present anything worthwhile. I feel convicted with the information I've been given. On one hand, I have no reason to not trust what William has told me. It is entirely possible that in a matter of weeks, our lands will cease to exist.

On the other hand, I do not know these people or their customs, and I'm likely being played for a fool so they have reason to declare war over us when the Queen's Heart does not turn up soon.

Thankfully, Callious always knows what to say when my head spins. It may be a while before I get a response, but hopefully, he can offer some helpful insight into the situation. At the very least, *someone* I know and trust will have the same information I've received.

Back in my room, I pull out my journal from the empty desk in the corner.

> Callious,
>
> I hope this finds you well. I've been in Oresteia for no more than a day, and I am already missing your presence. You always know what to say or do next when the opportunity presents itself. I have been bombarded by an overload of information already, and it leaves my head swimming.
>
> How are things there? How is your father? I've not met many people, but I have had the chance to make the acquaintance of Prince William and his cousin, Selene. Of course, King Kori is here too.
>
> The situation is potentially much more dire than anyone may know. Tell me, what is being whispered on that side of things? My journey was nothing short of eventful and magical. I hope to tell you more soon, though I fear I'm unallowed to speak of those things with those

not of my blood. The artifact presumably stolen
is one of great importance—to Oresteia and
Paralia. I still need to gain more

insight on how it all connects, but it is
possible that should this item not be delivered in
a reasonable time manner, things will cease
to be.

Again, I am doing my best to not speak out
of turn, should this end up in someone else's
hands. I still do not believe that any of the Frey
had to do with this disappearance, but I cannot
count it out either. I am unable to see what
either side has to gain by this circumstance, so
any insight you can offer would be appreciated.

Please, if you are able, tell me if you hear
anything. I am working on learning more here,
but that requires the time of Oresteia's prince,
who keeps being called off by his father. I don't
know if their many meetings have to do with
why I'm here, but I can't imagine what else
they'd be speaking about so urgently.

It feels wrong to be here without you. I feel
extremely underestimated by those around me,
but I will find a way to prove them wrong.

I will write more soon. I know you won't, but
don't tell father I wrote to you before I find the
chance to write to him.

May the sun guide you, P

Finishing my letter, I rip out the pages from my journal and fold them in half. After I've written Callious' name on top, I walk to Selene's door, intending to knock.

Before I get the chance to raise my fist, the door swings open, revealing a wide-eyed Selene.

"Penelope! I was just headed to dinner—would you like to join me?"

"If you could spare a few minutes to wait, I'd love to." I smile. "I came to ask if you had any sealing wax I could borrow. It seems my mind was not present when I packed my bag in Paralia."

She chuckles. "Probably because you had less than an evening to prepare for your departure. Let me grab mine for you—I believe I have extra to spare." Swiftly, her door shuts behind her as she disappears to grab the wax.

Just as quickly as she left, she's back with a handful of black sealing wax, a small candle, and a silver-plated wax holder.

Handing it over, she says, "I don't write many letters, so you can use all I have. If you need more, I know where we can find it."

"This is perfect. Give me one moment to finish sealing this letter, and I'd be delighted to share dinner with you." I take the items from her, heading back into my room.

I warm the wax in the holder and carefully pour it onto the edge of my letter. While it's still hot and pliable, I take my gold Frey family ring on my first finger and use it to stamp the wax.

Once it's cooled, I survey the picture depicted in

the wax's seal. The coast of Paralia is detailed, showing off the cliff's jagged edges in comparison to the sea's soft waves. Our palace is shown in the background in front of a sun so small you can hardly tell it's there.

In Paralia, we stamp our letters with gold wax, illuminating our golden coast. I find it very fitting that my first letter out of Oresteia is stamped with my family's signet but colored with the Pan family's wax.

One foot in each world—but for how long?

Sighing, I return everything to its rightful place within my desk and tuck the letter in my trouser pocket, hoping I can find someone to deliver this for me tonight. It's possible Selene would know a good person to ask.

Thinking of Selene reminds me that she is likely waiting for me to show up so she can go to dinner. I hurriedly check my reflection in the washroom's mirror and smooth down my curly hair.

Hand on the doorknob, I turn to check my room once more to make sure I have everything I need. Truthfully, I'm stalling. I don't know if dinner will be just me and Selene, or if there will be more of an audience. Exasperated, I shake the stress off my shoulders and turn the knob.

CHAPTER FOURTEEN

S ELENE STANDS ON THE OTHER SIDE OF MY DOOR, leaning against the adjacent wall with her leg kicked up behind her—a picture of graceful confidence. Her hair is pulled up, illuminating her high, pale cheekbones.

Seeing me, she immediately smiles and moves to walk toward me. "Did that wax work well for you?"

"Yes, it was just what I needed. Thank you."

"May I ask who you are writing to? Your father?"

Sheepishly, I smile and duck my head as we exit the hallway. "My best friend back home, Callious. I don't feel… confident enough… to write to my father. His expectations are much too high, and I cannot yet meet them."

She links her arm through mine, steering me toward the double doors I thought earlier must be for a dining room. The doors are now wide open, allowing me to peer in. A long table and chairs rest in the middle of the room, made of white marble and fitted with a black table runner down the middle.

Silver cutlery and dinnerware adorn the setting, set for four—even though this table could easily fit thirty. Tall white candlesticks are lit in the middle of the runner, paired with lamps along the walls, lighting up the rest of the vast space.

Selene laughs as we move to sit at the two places on the right side of the table. "Fathers are often like that. You *must* tell me all about Callious at once! I can send your letter off this evening with the head of our household staff if that would be acceptable to you."

"That would be exemplary." I sit, placing my black napkin on my lap. "As far as Callious goes, I'll tell you anything. What do you want to know?"

Selene finds the seat next to mine, mimicking my movement. As soon as she sits, a woman my mother's age rushes from the left side of the room with a pitcher of water in her hands.

Fitted in a black dress, it swishes at her ankles as she walks. Her silver-lined hair is pulled back in a bun, and her face looks both wise and youthful at the same time. She pours ice water into Selene's glass, not spilling a drop.

"Ah, Penelope, this is Tarsha. Tarsha, this is Penelope. Tarsha is the head server with our kitchen staff. She's been here as long as I can remember." I nod to Tarsha as she curtsies to me.

Selene laughs. "William and I used to convince Tarsha to give us extra servings of dessert as kids. She would wrap it for us in a spare napkin, allowing us a distraction so we could stow it away to our rooms when Kori wasn't looking."

Tarsha smiles, placing a gentle hand on Selene's cheek. Once the moment has passed, Tarsha fills my glass with ice water as well and moves to the side of the room once more. She places the pitcher on a silver rolling cart before disappearing behind the door to its left.

"That door connects to the kitchen. From the foyer, you can also access the kitchen through the door nearest to the left-hand staircase." Selene points in the general direction of that door. "Though, if you need anything, you only need to ask. There's never much of a reason to enter the kitchen ourselves."

"Tarsha seems very fond of you. Does she not often stay to chat?" I ask, taking a sip of my glass.

Selene smiles a bit sadly, checking to make sure no one else is presently standing in the room. "Tarsha isn't permitted to speak in our presence. Kori alone can give her consent to use her voice, but that does not happen very often. He believes there is no need for his staff to express themselves in that way."

I gasp, placing my hand on my chest in astonishment. "Does that not get lonely? I feel as though I would grow frustrated."

Selene shrugs, saying, "They are permitted to speak to each other, so long as we are not around. Tarsha used to sneak secret notes to William and I, placing them in our dessert-filled napkins."

She pauses. "They are well cared for here. Kori believes it's simpler this way—less opinions floating around."

"I suppose…" My voice trails off, not finishing the rest of my thoughts.

Just when I thought I was understanding a bit of Oresteia, something comes to throw me for a loop.

"So—Callious." She wiggles her eyebrows at me, leaning back in her chair to face me completely. "What does he do? Who is he?"

I laugh. "He's my best friend. Being the youngest of seven, you can imagine I'm not typically the first one they go to when they need someone." Absentmindedly, I grab the seashell necklace around my chest.

"Callious and I have known each other for seventeen years. His father is my family's favorite bladesmith. Everett, my oldest brother, took me to the shop to get my first dagger crafted for my upcoming fifth birthday. As we wandered waiting for Callious' father to come up front, I tripped on a loose tile on the floor."

I laugh, reminiscing on one of my earliest memories. "I fell into a shelf holding miscellaneous tools. Everett rushed over to grab the shelf, but as it wobbled, out walks Callious, ready to scold me for not being more careful. Instead, I think I caught him off guard by being the same age as him. He's been holding me together ever since."

I place my hand back in my lap. "He was training to be a bladesmith under his father's supervision, but before I left Paralia, he stated his intention to join the Kingdom's army. He asked me to go with him—to leave my crown behind."

Selene gapes at me and the meaning that phrase holds. "And you said no? Forgive me for speaking out of turn, but do you not… love him in that way?"

I nod, taking hold of my water glass again. "I said no. He is… as constant to me as Paralia's sun. But I didn't want to be left with thoughts of wondering if I could have helped, even though I did not know what I was getting myself into here. And, though I love him dearly, my family would never let anything in that regard happen between us—regardless of if I held a title or not."

She nods as servers stream out of the kitchen's door, bringing rolling carts to our places at the table. Portions of meat, potatoes, and vegetables are generously served to our plates. On the side, a slice of chocolate cake is placed next to my main dish.

As soon as the servers depart, Selene and I dig in. "What is this meat?" I ask between bites.

"I believe this is goat, but it could be lamb. I'm really very terrible at telling the difference. It's rare we get served anything other than those."

After a bit of silence stretches on, I peek to see if Tarsha, or anyone else, is beside the door. "So— magic." I wiggle my eyebrows back at Selene, causing a laugh to slip from her lips.

She waves her hand in the air, still holding onto her fork, and all the lamps and candles in the room extinguish at once. With a point, she alights a singular candle in front of me on the table. Picking up another piece of dinner, she uses her other hand to snap, and all the lights come back on.

Still as stunned as before, I ask, "How long have you been able to… do that?"

"At the age of ten, I was brought into the stronghold for the first time. My parents had just been killed —suffocated in the night by a neighbor hoping to gain access to the royal household." She takes a big bite of her cake, leaning her head back as if savoring the bite. "Instead, they gained access to the mountaintop—tied to a tree at the peak of Escaeus during one of our... bigger storms."

She pauses, chewing on her words. "At ten, I did not have anywhere else to go. Kori took me in immediately. While I'm still a niece and cousin, he declared me as part of the royal family. Overnight, I found myself with the ability to manipulate the flamed lights within the castle. Years of practice and experimentation have allowed me the capability to do what you've seen today."

"And what of William's magic?" I debate asking about her parents, but I do not want to unnecessarily make her uncomfortable by sharing that part of her heart with me.

She winks at me. "That's his story to tell." She wipes her mouth on her napkin, placing it in the center of her empty plate. "If you're finished, we can inquire regarding his whereabouts, if you'd like."

I smile, leaving my seat. "Honestly, if it's okay, I'm ready to retire for the evening." I take the letter out of my trousers, holding it out to her. "Would you be able to give my letter to the head of your household staff?"

"Of course! Let me walk you back." After taking the letter, she links arms with me again, steering me back toward the bedroom hall.

As she leaves me to retire, I smile to myself.

Even though a few of King Kori's tendencies are questionable, Selene and William have made me feel both comfortable and cared for within just a few days of being here.

Their hospitality makes my heart swell, allowing me to relish in the feeling of being welcomed somewhere.

I really enjoy their stories and their company. It feels so easy to fit in here.

But I still have so much more to learn and do.

CHAPTER FIFTEEN

UNLIKE YESTERDAY, I AWAKE TO GLOOMY, SNOWY SKIES. My room is edged with a chill in the air, beckoning me to stay under the warm covers of my bed. As I close my eyes once more, there's a sharp rap of knuckles on my room door.

Sitting up, I wait to see if the person on the other side of my door will announce themselves. After a moment of silence, the sound of paper gliding across the stone hits my senses.

There, just past the threshold, a small piece of paper lies on my floor. Footsteps recede from the other side of my door as I hop out of bed and dawn on the slippers awaiting me.

I pick up a note no bigger than my palm and read:

Breakfast?
—William

Scribbled hastily, the ink is smudged. I place the note on my desk and begin getting ready for the day, choosing a long-sleeved bright chalk-colored dress with the leather boots I wore yesterday. I grab my white cloak and braid my hair swiftly down my back, checking my reflection once before rushing out the door.

As I exit, I run right into Selene, coming from the end of the hall.

"Oh! I'm so sorry," I mumble, my cheeks growing warm with embarrassment.

"I was wondering if you were up yet. Where are you off to?" She asks, taking hold of my arms to steady myself.

She doesn't look off-balance at all.

"William invited me to breakfast; I didn't want to keep him waiting long."

"Ah, of course." She winks at me, letting go. "I will let you continue on your way then. I hope to see you later?"

"I'd love to." She retreats to enter her bedroom, leaving me behind in the hallway. I brush myself off and make my way back to the dining room.

▲▲▲

As soon as I enter the double doors, William's blue eyes fly to mine as he jumps out of his seat to pull out the chair next to him. "Penelope—just the person I was hoping to set eyes on this morning. I take it you received my mail?"

Moving to sit in the chair he's holding for me, I say, "Yes, though I did question whether or not I wanted to get out of bed yet. There was a chill in the air this morning, unlike anything I've felt before."

He releases my chair, sitting next to me again. At once, Tarsha is back, filling my glass and his with water. With that, she moves back into the kitchen, giving us privacy within the room.

William grabs his glass, holding it to his lips. His other arm finds its way around the back of my chair, leisurely resting there.

He eyes me as if debating what to say next. Swirling his water in his glass, he asks, "What was your most memorable birthday?"

I laugh, already having forgotten about his question stipulation from yesterday. I lean back, crossing my arms as if to ponder my answer. "I have two—is that permissible in your eyes?"

He smiles, an unspoken challenge crossing his gaze. "I would be delighted to hear as many as you'll speak."

"My earliest would be my fifth birthday. I received my first dagger—handcrafted by Callious' father. Lined with gold, the hilt is adorned with waves, winding around the grip to fit my fingers. The middle of the cross-guard holds a sun, shining a deeper gold than the rest of the dagger." I laugh. "Though it's customary for us to receive our daggers at five, typically we aren't allowed practice until our tenth birthday. I used to hide it under my pillow so I could practice wielding it in the middle of the night."

He raises an eyebrow at me, smiling. "And do you still wield a dagger?"

I shrug sarcastically, taking a sip from my glass. "When the occasion arises."

William laughs, removing his arm from behind my chair to run his hand through his hair.

"My other most memorable birthday would have to be when my father announced in front of my entire family that I would be leaving for an unknown amount of time to live in Oresteia." I raise my glass as if to toast. "*That* one left a mark on my memory."

William gapes, stunned. "You found out… on your birthday? Just a few days ago?"

I shrug, this time in defeat. "I'm not even sure my father remembered it *was* my birthday. Though, who can blame him—a lot was going on at the time."

William shakes his head and knocks back the rest of his water in one drink. He opens his mouth as if to respond, but shuts it, furrowing his eyebrows.

"Since it appears I have left you speechless, I believe it's my turn to ask *you* a question."

He smiles, gesturing outwardly with his arms, opening himself up from where he sits next to me. "I'm prepared for whatever you may have."

I ponder, wondering what sort of question I could ask to catch him off guard enough to give me more information about Oresteia and who the Pan family truly is.

As I think, the servers make their way out of the kitchen, placing food on our plates.

The smell of bacon and eggs fills my senses, drifting up with the hot steam pouring off my plate. A small bowl of gravy is placed next to my plate, just begging me to drown my meal in its flavor.

Tarsha comes back out with a steel pitcher this time, and the scent of coffee fills the room. She pours William a full mug, then looks to me as if to ask if I'd like some too. I smile, nodding yes.

As soon as she finishes, I take the mug to my lips, attempting a sip. The hot liquid rushes down my throat, warming me from the inside out.

The servers retreat to the kitchen, Tarsha with them, and William and I begin eating.

All of a sudden, I drop my fork, my question for William hitting me out of nowhere. Startled, he looks over his right shoulder and quirks his eyebrow up at me.

I smile, wiping my hands on the napkin next to my plate. Facing him fully, I wait for him to mimic my posture. Getting the hint, he pauses eating and holds my gaze.

"What magic do you hold?" I ask, adrenaline coursing through my veins. My heart beats so fast it feels as though it might erupt from my chest.

He grins knowingly as if he had guessed this might be what I would ask of him.

"Can you be trusted?"

My eyes widen and I stumble over my words. "Of... of course!"

His face turns serious as he looks at me with intention. "Penelope, should I show you, this new knowledge cannot leave Oresteia. Both Selene and my father know, but that is *it*. It's not to be spoken of, hinted at, or written about. You will have to lie to your family, your friends, and pretend you know nothing. Is that clear?"

Mentally, I debate with myself. But, at the back of

my mind, something calls to me, begging me to stop hiding in the shadows: unknowledgeable and unneeded.

I square my gaze with William's, whispering, "Show me."

CHAPTER SIXTEEN

WILLIAM CLAIMS THAT HE CANNOT SHOW ME HIS MAGIC until we finish our meal. Not sparing a second, I quickly down my breakfast, washing it down with the rest of my hot coffee. His bites are slower, unhurried as if to taunt me.

Once I've finished, I softly elbow him in the side, beckoning him to eat faster. He chuckles, and just as he wipes his hands on his napkin and begins to rise from his seat, Kori enters the dining room.

I freeze, having not seen him since he sent me off with Selene my first day. I glance at the table, my eyes finding a lone empty table placement that I didn't catch before.

William bristles beside me but places a cool mask over his features as he nods to his father. "Forgive us— we were just on our way out." He places a hand on my lower back, ushering me out of the room.

Behind us, Kori declares, "Take care, William, that you do not do too much."

"I wouldn't dream of it." William retorts, not issuing a single glance back. I, on the other hand, cannot help but look over my shoulder to Oresteia's King.

Kori stands next to the table, looking down his nose at us. His cold stare drifts down to where William's hand is still on my back, and I nervously step out of reach of his touch as we leave the dining room.

William passes me a glance as he takes his hand away, flexing his fingers before placing a tightly clenched fist at his side.

My face warms as I follow him to the right- hand side staircase, mentally cursing myself for allowing Kori's look to bother me so much.

My heart is torn. I'm growing to like William, but there is so much I still do not know about this place. Should I grow to love Oresteia, and even though nothing will ever move forward between Callious and me, I still feel obligated to belong to Paralia's shores with him by my side as it always has been.

I do not fear change, but I am scared of ruining chances for things to stay the same if that's how they are meant to be.

Though the tide may shift the shore, the tide remains unchanging.

Lost in my own world, I hardly notice that William has led me back to the room where his piano is placed. Shutting the door behind us, he goes to light all the lamps within this space, rather than just the one in the corner like last time.

"I thought you preferred the door open when you play?" I ask, moving to follow him around the room.

"Ah, but I will not merely just be playing in this instance. Rather, playing these keys will accompany what happens next." As I trail behind, he walks behind the heavy black curtain, lifting the lid off the piano and sitting on the bench.

I stand just behind him, unsure of where I should go for this display. I wring my hands in front of me, hesitating.

William turns to look at me, the room's lighting placing harsh shadows across his face. In the dark of this space, he looks more like his father. And yet, his ice-colored eyes hold a softness there that Kori's never will.

"I can give you one more chance to walk away, lest you be tempted to share this with someone else." He pauses, searching for his next words. "Such as Callious."

I furrow my eyebrows, confused. "What do you know of Callious, other than what I've spoken?"

"I know enough." A muscle in his jaw twitches as he grinds his teeth together, as if in restraint from saying more.

I huff, annoyed. "Callious is not privy to all my secrets. I would not dare break your trust in such a regard."

He nods, his face relaxing with the intensity of my words. As William releases an exhale, his head falls back, eyes searching for something in the ceiling's stone. I study the expression on his face from what I can see—anguish and… uncertainty?

I place a hand softly on his left shoulder. "You can trust that this will not leave this room." I pause, searching for something else I can say to reassure him. "I…"

"Penelope, you do not have to try so hard." He quirks a smile at me over his shoulder. "I'm centering myself, to make it easier to call upon the magic within me."

I duck my head, embarrassed. Removing my hand from his shoulder, I allow myself to sit beside him on the bench, awaiting further instruction.

"For a moment, I need you to close your eyes." As I do, he continues, his voice a song I'm not ready to have end. "Picture somewhere you long to be. Imagine a world at your disposal in whatever way you wish."

As I dream, he begins to play. The piano begins soft, and light. I see a sun peeking through the clouds like a warm spring morning, mist covering the rays that touch my skin.

As the melody picks up, so does my imagination. The haziness of the sky now covers a range of snowy mountains, much like the ones I have outside my window. Flakes of snow and ice drift in front of my senses, teasing me with their soft touch.

William's music reaches a crescendo, and I imagine I'm standing on a snowy bank between peuko trees, their evergreen needles drifting in the breeze. The scent of pine and mint tickles my nose, begging me to take a deep breath of crisp mountain air.

I sigh, finding that this place within my mind feels like a mix of Paralia and Oresteia—a clash of warmth and chill bleeding together like old friends.

The piano's sound slows, finding a gentler tempo. "Open your eyes, Penelope," William whispers.

I peek, afraid of what I might see. My eyes grow wide as I look at the scene before me—exactly what I had pictured in my mind's eye. I am no longer sitting in a lamp-lit room hidden within a mountain.

I am standing on a cliff, overlooking the mountain range as snow falls and lands in my hair. The cold air whisks past me, requiring me to pull my cloak tight against my body as I feel a chill that creeps down to my bones.

I reach out a hand, touching the sharp needles of the peuko trees next to me. Upon closer inspection, I find brown colored cones hanging from the branches. Taking a step forward to grab one, I look down abruptly as the snow beneath my boots crunches as I walk.

Slowly, I spin, surveying my surroundings in a full 360-degree turn. Everywhere my eyes touch, I find no fault in this dreamlike world. There are no longer lamps lit amongst the wall, but a sun peeking through the gloom. The stone-carved walls do not exist, and in their stead, I find open mountain air.

William's piano has suddenly vanished, though I can still hear his song traveling to me through the wind.

Stuttering, I try to find something to say, some way to call out to him. My voice is lost in the breeze, not able to be carried past the mountain's peak.

A snowflake touches my cheek, leaving a cold mark in its wake. I reach up to feel it and a bit of cold water brushes my fingertips.

Suddenly, the music stops, and I am once again sitting on the piano's bench to William's left, staring open-eyed at the wall furthest from me. My eyes readjust to the dimness of the room. My cloak is suddenly too hot to wear inside, the feeling of the fleece too tight around my neck.

I look down at my boots, finding no trace of snow on their soles. My head feels dry, and not a single bit of snow is found within my curly hair.

"What was that?" I gasp, still wide-eyed at the abrupt change in scenery.

William places the piano lid back upon the keys, facing me with apprehension. "Do you recall when I first brought you here how I said I had begun drifting toward music very early on in life?"

I nod. Before continuing, he reaches up to where the snowflake had touched my cheek, wiping its remains away, as if it was the only thing that truly happened.

"We didn't understand what was happening at first. I would hum a tune, play a key, and suddenly my father's innermost desires would begin playing out in front of our eyes. The longer I sang or played, the more detailed and immersive the scenery would become."

He shakes his head. "You can imagine that a man of my father's caliber does not particularly enjoy his most private thoughts becoming a reality, even in front of just his son."

"So," he continues, "we carved out this space. I taught myself piano; I hid away behind this curtain. I've learned how to expand the illusions so that it touches every sense. I've disciplined myself so that I only create these illusions when *I* desire, rather than every time I sing or play a note."

He looks down at his hands, now speaking quieter. "And they are not always… pleasant… illusions. I am no stranger to making someone's worst nightmare come true to get them to do what needs to be done."

I place a hand on his own, willing him to look back up at me. As we make eye contact, I smile softly. "I'd grown tired of Paralia." I confess.

He smiles back, his eyes twinkling, no longer completely ashamed. Rather, he looks confused at my confession. "I assumed you loved your Kingdom."

I sigh. "It's not that I do not love Paralia, or aspects of its sunny exterior, but it's always the same. There is no rain, no snow, no cloud cover. The days are long, bright, and hot. I often prayed to the sun that it might offer me reprieve—that it might give me something new."

I pause. "It never has. Coming here has been a gift in that way. If it were up to me, I might choose to never go back. I think that's why your illusion showed me what it did. Could you see it too?"

He smiles at me, seeming to understand the longing and conviction behind my words. "Yes."

"Good." I squeeze his hands before returning mine to my lap. "And thank you."

CHAPTER SEVENTEEN

WILLIAM LEAVES SOON AFTER FOR A MEETING HE IS TO attend. Before he left, he had someone send for Selene, since she had expressed she wanted to see me later today.

The chill in my bones has not completely relented, and I feel the cold air calling to me as I walk. I'm hoping Selene is willing to escort me outside. Now that I'm fully properly dressed, I think a walk in the snow would be delightful.

I wander to the foyer once more, finding the windows that line the wall adjacent the front doors. Flurries of snow drift down, beckoning me. After William's illusion, I have a desire deep within me to experience all that was tangible in real life.

Heels click on the tile behind me, and Selene comes to stand to my left.

"How are there windows if we are inside Escaeus?" I ask, not bothering to have my gaze leave the window.

"The entire mountain has been carved out to

create the stronghold. Where there is a glass pane, there once was a hole crafted into the side of the mountain for this purpose. Though, you can imagine that would be tedious. That's why there are not many."

She nods back toward the royal hall. "Your room and mine are the only bedrooms that have windows. Yours is by far the biggest."

"How does that work with the outside world? Surely people notice a piece of glass cut into the mountain's side?"

She waves her hand nonchalantly, as if all of this is merely small talk. "The glass was crafted so that from the outside, it looks as if the mountain is whole. No one can see in, but we can see out." She looks around, leaning forward to be closer to me. "Magic," she whispers.

I laugh, the sound echoing in the empty foyer.

"What would you like to do this afternoon? I have no pressing matters to attend to." Selene runs her long ponytail through her fingers, flipping it over her shoulder.

"Would I be permitted to go outside? I haven't seen much of the stronghold, or the area surrounding it. If I'm to be here for a while, I'd like to get to know this place in its entirety."

"I'd love to take you. We can go to the garden now if you'd like—I need to take some time for target practice anyhow. If you want to change into trousers, I'll grab us some sandwiches from the kitchen and a guard to accompany us."

She starts to walk away, but I call to her, confused, "What sort of target practice?"

She looks over her shoulder at me and winks, a portrait of cool authority. "Bring your dagger."

▲▲▲

Once I've dressed the part, I wrap my dagger's leather belt around my waist. Dark green in color, it sharply contrasts the stark white of my outfit. I wrap my hair in a ponytail, thinking it should help keep it out of my face while the wind blows.

As I go to grab my cloak once more from the closet, I find an article of clothing that was not present before.

A thick-layered coat hangs in the front of the rack, white in nature. A hood falls off the back of the coat, the interior covered in a soft light gray fleece. Around the hanger, a cream-colored note is suspended, as if the writer punctured it through the hanger's wire at the last minute.

I rip it from where it hangs and read:

I was told you weren't given a coat.
Take mine.
—William

I shake my head, laying the note to the side so I can fit the coat onto my body. The fleece immediately warms me so much more than my cloak would, covering me from neck to hip. My sleeves are puffy and long, but fitted to my arms to keep my body heat in.

I walk to stand in front of my bathroom mirror and zip the coat shut, buckling the top layer over as well.

I look ridiculous.

I giggle, fixing my dagger so that it is hidden beneath the coat's layers. As I peer into the mirror, I'm surprised at the sparkle present in my eyes and the rosy color of my cheeks as I smile at my reflection.

I look like I could be happy here.

A sadness touches my heart as I realize that will never be fully true. I will have to go back when this is all over—whether to live out my days in my sibling's shadows, or in preparation for the war to come. Either way, it will be Paralia that has me, not Oresteia.

I do not look back or think twice as I leave to meet with Selene again, squaring my shoulders once more.

▲▲▲

Selene is standing in the foyer wearing head to toe white gear for the first time since I've met her. Slung across her back is a wooden bow, the string hanging around her chest.

Standing next to her is a man I recognize from the guard post station when we entered Escaeus. Still decked out in all black, he looks less menacing standing here than he did in the shadows of the mountain.

"Penelope, Haldor. Haldor, Penelope." Selene introduces us, gesturing between him and I.

Haldor bows at the waist. "It's nice to finally make your acquaintance, Penelope." As he rises, I make note of his sharp facial features and shorn dark hair.

Now that I can see him in the light, he looks to be my brother Everett's age. He gives off a rugged nature, and I glance down at his hands to confirm that his knuckles are riddled with scars—worn and split with use.

"Enough with the introductions," Selene states, already making her way out of the foyer to climb the right-hand staircase.

Haldor gestures that I should go first, leaving him to trail behind us. I follow Selene to the first wooden door on the right. She opens it, revealing cold winter air on the other side.

"That door leads out?" I gasp. I never would have guessed their back door exit was on the second floor. "William told me it was a meeting room!"

She grins, knowing exactly what I'm thinking. "Pretty sneaky, huh?" She elbows me lightly, angling her head toward the door. "Follow me!"

As we leave the stronghold, I realize I am so glad I put on pants. The skirt of my dress would have been soaked within minutes of our journey.

The snow has drifted against the door, creating a deep draft right where we are walking. As we move along, it thins out, creating a path to follow. Haldor moves silently behind us, trailing us like a shadow.

"I noticed you're wearing white," I smirk, raising my voice above the wind so it reaches Selene in front of me.

"I'm not permitted to wear red when I go outside —too noticeable." Her gloved hand waves in the air flippantly.

We trek on for a few more minutes in silence,

passing peuko trees, getting snowed on, and almost being blown over by the wind a time or two.

Each step leaves an imprint, our boots sinking slightly with every stride. Our silence is broken only by the soft crunch of our footsteps and the occasional creak of branches overhead.

I go back and forth from watching where I step so as to not fall into a snow pile, and placing my eyes on the mountainscape looming in front of me. The white powder crunches beneath my feet as I walk, occasionally slipping beneath me as it turns into ice.

The trees break, creating a gap in front of my eyes. There, in the middle of the meadow, three targets of various distances stand. The closest target appears to be made of wood, with the target painted over the board.

Selene looks at me over her shoulder, peering at me from head to toe. "Have you ever thrown your dagger against a harsh wind, Penelope?"

CHAPTER EIGHTEEN

Selene walks to a large wooden chest underneath the tree next to where I stand. As she unclasps the lock and opens the lid, my eyes catch on what is hidden within: daggers, swords, arrows, bows, javelins. All fashioned in gold, these weapons appear to be basic and mostly untouched.

Selene grabs a red leather bag out of the chest full of arrows. Her name is printed on the bag strap, claiming it as her own. Each arrow shaft and fletching are thin and black—contrasting sharply to the gold tip of the arrow's head.

She removes the bow from around her chest and slings the quiver over her right shoulder. Selene moves back to the middle of the entryway, putting power into her confident stance.

Grabbing an arrow from her quiver, she nocks it quickly, placing it into the groove of her bow almost immediately.

She plucks at her bow string, holding it with her first three fingers, the arrow in between her first finger and the other two.

Pulling the string taut, she looks down the arrow at the furthest target, all while relaxing her hand's grip and shoulders.

She takes a deep breath and releases the arrow. Whistling through the mountain air, it hits the target board with a sharp *snap* directly in the middle of the bullseye.

Selene flips her ponytail over her shoulder to look at me smugly. "Your turn."

I laugh, thinking she's kidding. The gleam in her eye turns serious as her stare continues unwavering. "Show me what you're made of, *Paralia*. This is your chance to show off."

"I don't have anything to show, *Oresteia*." I retort. "I used to practice wielding my dagger in the middle of the night. Apart from basic blocking and parrying, I was not permitted to master this craft. I can't do *that*." I wave my hand toward the targets, gesturing wildly.

She smirks, slinging her bow back over her chest. "Well then, let's learn, shall we?"

▲▲▲

After grabbing me a bow and quiver of arrows from the chest, Selene coaches me through how to stand and hold my shoulders.

"We need to figure out which eye is your dominant

eye. You're right-handed?" I nod. "Look at that tree just past us. Stretch out your right hand and point at it with your finger."

I follow along to her instructions, placing my sight on the tree not more than ten feet from me.

"Continue to stare at the tree, but close your right eye." She pauses. "Now switch and look with your left eye only."

I oblige, not understanding the point of this. "With which eye open did your finger continue to point at the tree?"

"Uh," I begin, flipping back and forth between my two eyes now—opening one, closing the other. "I think my left eye?"

"Perfect. When you draw back your bowstring, that's the eye you'll want to keep open as you aim. That will help you be as precise as possible."

She gestures for me to practice my stance again, kicking at my boot for me to widen my feet to be shoulder width. I square my shoulders to be perpendicular to the target closest to where we are standing.

As Selene slowly circles my stance, my arms begin to shake. This bow is particularly heavy, and I'm not used to holding something like this for a long period of time.

"Drop your elbow just a bit."

I do, feeling sweat begin to crawl down my back. *William's coat is extremely insulated.*

"Good. Now look down the shaft and aim at the target. There's no breeze yet, so you don't need to account for any of that here."

I look down my arrow, keeping my left eye open. A curl begins to unravel in front of my face, and I try to blow it out of the way.

"Use your back, not your arm, to keep your arrow steady." She taps between my shoulder blades, which helps me focus on those muscles instead.

"When you're ready, take a deep breath, and release. As you release your fingers from the string, allow your right arm to follow through backward. Continue to hold your left arm firm as your arrow goes toward the target."

I shake my head, repeating her words mentally.

Who would have thought shooting an arrow would require this many steps?

I take a deep breath, centering myself. I can feel her sharp stare permeating through my heavy winter gear. As I exhale, I release my arrow, following Selene's instruction.

My arrow shoots quickly out of the bow, but only makes it about halfway to the closest target before plummeting to the ground.

I smile sheepishly at her, my face growing warm with embarrassment as she walks to pick the arrow up.

"You need to pack on some muscle, girl."

I laugh, taking the arrow from her. "You think?"

▲▲▲

We practice a few more times, making minor adjustments each time I shoot. Unfortunately, the arrows do not make it any further than my first one did. As I walk around the clearing to retrieve them all, Selene asks Haldor to break out our lunch.

I lay my bow and quiver back into the chest to keep them from getting wet on the snowy ground and take my wrapped sandwich from Haldor.

My stomach rumbles as I unwrap the fresh bread from the parchment. Piled high with meat, cheese, and veggies, I'm practically drooling by the time I lift the sandwich for my first bite.

"I don't think I've ever had a sandwich this good," I mumble between bites.

"It's crazy how hungry a little practice makes you. I'm always starving when I leave this area to go back to the stronghold."

"How often do you come out here?"

"Every day, if I'm able." Selene finishes her sandwich extremely quickly, handing her empty wrapper back to Haldor. "My head is able to be completely empty when I'm present here. I was taught archery at a very young age by my father. It keeps me grounded and connected to him, even though he is gone."

She pauses, toying with the snow on the ground with a gloved hand next to where we sit on a fallen log.

"As I grow older, I bear more responsibility. I don't think Kori likes that I still practice, hoping for a chance to earn my way into the royal guard. He will never let me, but I do believe William would, if given the chance."

"Why won't Kori allow you to enter the guard? Surely they need someone as talented as you with a bow and arrow."

She scoffs at my question. I crumple my empty

sandwich wrapper amidst the silence, handing it to Haldor who is just behind us, standing watch.

"Kori believes I would be a liability. We've been fighting over it for years—ever since I turned of age to join at fifteen. There is no question I'm the best archer the guard would have, but he claims that it would demoralize his male soldiers to have me join."

She sighs. "He thinks if they believe me to be competition, some may attempt to remove me out of spite. Kori does not want to have to break up a civil war within his own army. Especially now that his sights are set on Paralia." Selene winces. "No offense."

I shrug off her comment, moving past it. "Surely he knows no one would be able to best you. I know I've only been here a few days, but I truly believe if you had opposition, you would be the one to fear, not them."

A soft smile aligns along her lips. "You would be right. But he will never be swayed. William's crowning will be my only shot at doing what I want." Her gloves brush her pants, knocking the snow off her palms. "We should start heading back—it looks like it'll be an early evening tonight."

I stop her as she rises to leave. "Will we be able to come back another day? I'd like to attempt throwing my dagger."

"If that's something you'd like to pursue, I'm sure William would be more than happy to accompany you. Dagger throwing isn't within my particular skill set."

I sigh, disappointment filling my mind. It feels as though I'm always promised one thing but given another.

The sun knows William and I have many other things on our plate to discuss, particularly regarding the Queen's Heart.

Haldor speaks up from behind us, his voice gruff and firm. His gaze is on the horizon, peering intently at the clouds covering the sunless sky. "It's time to go."

CHAPTER NINETEEN

The way back is filled with an unspoken silence as we trudge our way through the snow. The temperature drops as we walk, requiring me to mentally give thanks for William's coat wrapped around my body.

We enter the stronghold the same way we left—through the second story door. Haldor seals it behind us and makes his way back to the foyer without a word or second glance.

"He's a man of few words, I suppose?" I question as Selene and I kick the ice off our boots.

"He must have sensed something in the air. He's typically more fun than that—it's why he's my favorite guard to take with me when I go."

We make our way downstairs back toward the royal hall. Intending to change, I step toward my own room as Selene moves toward hers. As we part,

William flings open his own bedroom door, stretching his neck out the doorway to find us.

He makes eye contact with me as he leaves his

room, his eyes surveying me from head to toe. Something in his smirk makes me both shiver and blush at the same time. Rather than ducking my gaze as I'm accustomed, I challenge his stare and keep my eyes locked with his.

Two can play this game.

After what feels like minutes, Selene clears her throat from where she's standing in her bedroom's threshold. "William, did you *need* something? We're cold."

His electric-blue eyes blink, as if he forgot where he was standing and what he was doing. Reclaiming a cool mask over his features, he leans against the wall of the hall, arms crossed over his chest in a perfect picture of indifference.

"The stronghold is going on lockdown for the evening. A storm is brewing, and the guards are restless. I was curious to know if Penelope would be willing to spend some time in the library with me to pour over some important matters?" He raises his eyebrow at me, mischief sparkling in his eyes.

Selene huffs, flipping her ponytail over her shoulder. "And where is *my* invitation?"

"If you believe you have anything to add to the conversation, be my guest," he bites back at her, his tone playful.

She rolls her eyes at him. "I'll be in the bath if you need me." She turns to leave, but looks over her shoulder at him one last time. "Please, don't need me."

Her bedroom door shuts with a click, leaving William and I standing in the hall.

"Would you *also* like to be unneeded this evening?" He asks, moving closer to where I'm standing.

"That depends… is that your question for me?" I taunt.

He laughs, his head flinging back with the sound. "It can if you want it to be, but I feel as though that's rather boring." He reaches out a hand to tuck a wayward curl behind my ear. His hands are so warm and soft against my cheek that I have to resist the urge to lean into his touch.

"I'll allow you another question, but I get to choose which I answer."

He ponders this, leaning his head on the wall to his right. As his gaze wanders toward the ceiling, I allow myself to stare at the scar I noticed once before, just under his left eye.

The mark is faded and raised, no longer than my pinky finger. White in color, it does not contrast against his pale skin from far away, but up close, it's noticeably different. I want to take off my glove and run my finger across its jagged edge, but I fear my cold hand would be too much.

I feel the weight of his stare back on me, and I lift my eyes to meet his. I had not realized how closely we stood—as if just a breath separates us.

When he finally breaks the silence, his voice is low, as if to not ruin the moment. "Do you like gifts?" His eyes bounce back and forth between my own, as if he cannot choose where to place his gaze.

I swallow, nervousness coating my tongue. "Yes." I manage, my voice stuck in my throat.

"Yes, you like gifts?" He pauses, leaning his right

arm above my head against the wall. His head is much closer to mine, our noses almost touching. "Or yes, you'd like to be unneeded this evening?" He grins.

I laugh, the trance we were in now broken. I act as if I'm thinking long and hard regarding that answer, humming as I move my eyes around and mimic his nonchalant stance against the wall.

He lightly shoves me in the shoulder, causing me to laugh.

"Yes, William, I like gifts." I absentmindedly go to touch my necklace from where it lays on my chest.

William's eyes catch the movement, eyebrow raising at the potential meaning behind it. I drop my hand before he can ask questions, volunteering the information to him instead.

"Being the youngest, I can't recall many times where I was given something that wasn't owned by my sibling first. My dagger, and this necklace, are the only two things that come to mind that I received firsthand." I explain.

He mulls that over, obviously distraught at the thought. I suppose that being the only child, and a prince no less, he's never *not* received anything firsthand.

Hoping to redeem the moment, I quickly ask, "Where did you get your scar?"

He looks taken aback for a second and reaches up to touch the healed wound. "That is one of my favorite stories." He grins, his eyes sparkling.

"When I was young, about nine, my father was invited to a meeting of sorts. At that age, I had just lost my mother. My magic was very early in its stages, and father believed that if he took me with him, I might begin to learn the stake of my role."

He pauses as his gaze softens, looking down at me. "There was a girl there about my same age. She was fiery—running around with no shoes, her hair flying behind her in knots. I remember standing there after introductions in my crisp white attire, baffled at how carefree she moved.

"I felt as though if I breathed the wrong way, father would invoke discipline. But there she was, dancing with the wind, begging me to play with her."

He laughs as he recalls the rest of his story. Entranced, I hang onto every word, envisioning the girl that captivated his attention so young.

"I did. We ran, laughed, and rolled around. By the time my father was done with his meeting, my white clothes were covered in grass stains and my hair was disheveled. The logistics of the meeting did not go well. My father stormed out of their palace. The realization of what I had done to myself hit me, and fear overtook my body."

Shaking his head, he continues, "We were playing catch with a rock. I had just taunted her, telling her she threw like a girl. In the same moment my father came rushing out of their home, she had thrown the rock. It hit me under the eye, cutting across the soft skin of my cheek. All because I was no longer paying attention to her, but to him."

My eyes land back on his scar as he finishes his story. "My father grabbed me by the wrist, stating we were leaving that instant. I looked back at her, catching a glimpse of her apologetic face as blood ran down my cheek."

Softly, I ask, "What happened to her?"

He sighs. "I didn't know for a long time. A few years ago, my father let me into the reason behind that meeting, filling me in on everything that should have happened and everything that didn't. I've been looking for her ever since."

I smile, a knot forming in my stomach. I don't know why his fondness for her is making my chest tight.

It must be the cold getting to me.

"Thank you for telling me," I say. "If you'll allow me a few minutes to change, I'd love to accompany you to the library. On the account that there's coffee waiting for us, of course."

He laughs, taking a step backward from where we stood. The space between us now feels like a gaping hole. "Of course."

CHAPTER TWENTY

William and I part ways, stating he will send for coffee and meet me in the library. Now that I have time to rejuvenate, I peel off my wet layers in the bathroom and lower myself into the hot bath.

My upper body is extremely sore from archery practice—even though I've only barely begun—and the scalding water relaxes my muscles as I sink into the tub.

After quickly scrubbing my body head to toe and using every drop of warm water there is, I find a pair of soft linen pants and a sweater to match. My bare feet are warm against the stone, and I wonder if there's a heating element beneath the room's floor.

I dawn on thick socks and a pair of slip-on shoes. I attempt to rebraid my wet hair on my way out, but my curls are not fully cooperating with me. Towel drying my soaked locks in the messy braid one last time, I rush out the door and head upstairs to the library.

▲▲▲

The four flights of stairs cause me no trouble as I take them two at a time, my years spent racing Callious back up from the coastline allowing me to be in the right shape.

I feel a pang in my heart as I think about the absence of my best friend, and I wonder when he will write. It's only been a day since I gave my letter to Selene to send off, but because of Oresteia's nature, I am hopeful it will arrive in Paralia quicker than a normal letter might.

William is sitting at the table in the middle of the room, the fireplace blazing behind him. He sips on a mug with his back perpendicular to me, reclining in his chair with his feet on the table.

As soon as I enter, he sets his mug down and plants his feet back on the floor. Gesturing to the seat beside him, I follow his wishes and sit.

"I believe I'm entitled to ask another question, as this is a separate time of seeing you today," he states.

"I suppose I can allow that." I shrug as I adjust to get comfortable in the wooden chair, allowing my arms to rest on the table in front of me as I lean in.

His bright stare feels as though it's permeating into my very soul as he considers his question carefully.

Though I wasn't sure at first what I thought, I do enjoy this little game we play. Something about him feels so familiar in the way we converse and banter. It feels as though I could have known him my whole life, and I wonder what would be if I had.

I wonder what could have been if Oresteia and Paralia hadn't been in strife most of my life. Especially now, with the accusations that are thrown around constantly, I don't know what will come of our two Kingdoms.

A small part of me hopes that as I travel back to Paralia, William and I might stay in touch. Now that I know the way, I might be permitted to travel back and forth and even see Selene on occasion.

As Everett grows closer to taking the throne and crown, surely he would not mind me acting as ambassador to Oresteia. If anything, he might find it helpful as William assumes his own crown to have someone who has lived in their shoes.

Of course, that is only if we can find the Queen's Heart.

My stomach turns. The stakes are so high, and I'm sitting here imagining a world that may never exist.

William clears his throat, gaining my attention once again. I refocus on him and find him eyeing me with suspicion.

"Where did you go?"

"Is that your question?" I ask, confused.

"It is. Where did you go, just now?" He leans in, whispering those words to me softly.

Embarrassed, I respond, "I was imagining what life might be like should we recover what's been lost." I pause, a lump caught in my throat. "I wonder if I might be permitted to stay in touch, or to visit, once I've set foot back on Paralia's shores."

He nods, a silence looming between us. My heart beats fast as he considers his response.

"And what, might I ask, would you want life to look like?" He gives me a soft grin, as if he might be guessing my train of thought.

He's distracting—the way the fire dances off his sharp cheekbones and bright features. His white-blonde hair looks as if it's ablaze in this light, softly laying over his forehead, as if he couldn't be bothered to do a thing to it this morning.

"I believe I might be able to be of help once my brother takes the crown." I swallow, my tongue heavy in my mouth. "That maybe I could be an emissary of sorts as you both ascend to rule."

William ponders this, and the silence leaves me aching for the sound of his voice.

"Is that all? You seemed far off in thought for quite some time." He props an elbow on the table, leaning his chin into his palm as he looks at me with an eyebrow raised.

Sparks dance in his eyes, mischief playing within his gaze.

"I believe you've asked enough questions." I wink and he throws his head back in laughter, the sound echoing off the bookshelves among us.

"Fair enough. And what do *you* want to ask *me*?"

"Do you like me?" I blurt, not meaning to say it quite so aggressively.

His smile broadens, radiating in amusement. "Well, yes, Penelope, I suppose you could claim I *like* you."

"I mean…" I hesitate. "Do you consider me… a friend?"

William leans forward to tuck a wayward curl behind my ear. His hand lightly finds my chin, pulling it up to make me fully meet his eyes. He tucks my hair so often it feels as though he is looking for an excuse to touch me.

"Do you want to be my friend, Penelope?" His voice is low, causing goosebumps to jump along my arms.

"Yes…" I trail off, unsure of where to go from here. "I just thought I might ask, so I could know where your intentions lie."

He chuckles softly. "And what do you think my intentions are?"

Still holding my chin, his thumb begins to lightly brush my jaw.

I shiver, trying to maintain eye contact. "To be honest, I'm not sure." I laugh, trying to cover up my nervousness. "Although anything more may be… inappropriate given the current status between our Kingdoms."

His eyes linger on mine, the blue of his eyes taking a darker tone as his jaw clenches, a muscle ticking in disappointment. William takes his hand away from my face, righting his posture to create space between us.

"Besides the strife between our two worlds, is there anything—or anyone—you have in mind that might prove 'more' to be difficult?" He crosses a leg, resuming a position of confidence.

I wish I could return the feeling.

I grab my shell necklace, thinking of my devotion for Callious, though I do not know how to explain that nothing will ever be permitted to happen between him and me. William tracks the movement, nodding to himself as his eyes watch where my hand falls.

"Understood," he says. Abruptly, he stands from his chair, walking around the room collecting an abundance of books from various places.

I sigh, feeling defeated. My intention was not to put him off, but rather get a read on our situation. Though, it's probably for the best that we do not waste time away with stolen glances and soft touches, knowing what is at stake for both of us.

And yet, I still cannot help but wonder.

A ball of regret forms in my stomach, causing a shift in my mood. Annoyance makes way and breaks the surface of my mind, causing my nose to crinkle in defiance.

Why do I care so much about what he thinks?

My eyes follow his movement as he brings a stack of books back toward our table.

He drops the books on the surface. "Let's begin."

CHAPTER TWENTY-ONE

Sitting in silence, we pour over book after book, looking for information on the Queen's Heart and the background behind it.

The library is illuminated by a warm glow as we sit deeply engrossed in the books before us. My finger traces lines of text as I scan each page with focus.

I cannot find anything that contradicts what William had told me—that the Heart came from the Tree because of the blood pact made long ago. But I also fail to find new information.

Periodically, we exchange murmured observations or shared discoveries, our voices hushed and clipped short. The rustle of turning pages fills the quiet atmosphere.

Letting my mind wander, I begin to think of the specifics of the information he had offered me.

I break the quiet by saying, "Do you think the enchantment around the Queen's Heart would allow someone of accepted status to break in and take it?

Much like how the Janus Tree tests your intentions and allows one with royal approval through?"

He ponders while I continue. "If the Queen's Heart came from the Janus Tree, surely they play by the same rules."

He looks up from the book in front of him, making eye contact with me for the first time since we started reading.

"That could be." He scratches the top of his head. "If that's the case, could it be true that the magic that flows in Oresteia from it might bleed into the heart of any other royal? Perhaps, one from Paralia?"

I lean forward in shock, accidentally knocking a book off the table. "You think I might have magic?"

"I think the Queen's Heart got up and walked away—anything is possible at this moment," he says pointedly, closing his book.

"Let's run back through what you told me—what we know. Maybe there's something there we can use to hypothesize where it may have gone."

He laughs, and I'm thankful to have gotten a rise out of him once again. I don't enjoy the tension we've been sitting in for the last few hours, and I hope to not repeat that incident.

No matter what, I hope we are always able to stand on the same ground.

"Okay. I was always told the casing surrounding the Queen's Heart is enchanted as to not let anyone without royal blood to open it. What exactly did my father tell you about the Janus Tree?"

I think back on that conversation from days ago, trying to recall Kori's exact words. "He said that someone must have the stamp of the Kingdom marked into their skin to enter. Though, I don't completely understand what that means. Could it be a branding?"

"That seems intense. Maybe a wax seal on their person? Verbal affirmation from a King?"

I nod, mulling over those options. "For the sake of the question, let's assume all are true. Does the enchantment then also test a person's intentions?"

"You would think, but it's not something quite as dire as passage between the Kingdoms. Maybe that means the stakes aren't quite as high for this instance. And are we considering it impossible to hide your true intentions from something?"

I ponder. "I suppose if the enchantment deems your intentions more important than staying tucked away in casing, it might let you through."

"What does that mean of the guard that should have been on duty? We talked to the guards on rotation that day—no one was late to their post, and none saw anything amiss."

"And you trust them all to be true to their word?"

He nods intently. "They would not be trusted with guarding the Queen's Crown if not."

"What does the throne room look like? Could there be a back passage perhaps? Somewhere someone could sneak in and out?" I chew on my lip, my book long forgotten in my lap.

He thinks before saying, "I have explored every inch of this castle—there is certainly a secret passage or two. Though, we'd have to thoroughly search each to find if it connects to the throne room specifically."

"Okay…" I pause. I feel like the answer is right on

top of us, the hypothetical bleeding to be true. "You told me the jewel was replaced? How long do you think it had been before you found it was fake?"

He gets up and starts to pace the room, his brain going miles a minute, his tongue hardly able to keep up. "We believe it had been three months before we retrieved you. Our magic slowly degenerated, and my father and I tried to trace back to a possible starting date."

"What tipped you off?" I ask, watching him run his fingers through his hair.

"My father had trouble using his magic one day. It was to the point that he could not control it as he wished, so we investigated it. The jewel was slightly askew in the Crown, not quite the right fit." He stops. "I believe the fake jewel was put back so no one would suspect anything."

"So, what can we do? Is there someone within your city that might know who crafted it and how?"

He shakes his head. "We asked, and nothing concrete was given to us. That's why father went forward with assuming it had been a Frey."

I nod, understanding. I had started to think they had begun with accusing us, rather than looking internally at themselves first. I'm grateful they at least started with the process of demanding answers.

I don't plan on forsaking that process.

"I think I need to see the throne room, in order to get a better lay of the land and what may have happened."

William looks at me.

"I suppose I'll lead the way."

CHAPTER TWENTY-TWO

We put all the books back in their rightful places, and I'm tempted to find a book or two I'd like to keep with me when I go back to my room.

I've never been much of a reader, but I blame that on the books I was forced to read growing up.

Because I was not often let in on the important lessons and discussions that my other siblings took part in, I was given a lot of books to read to compensate for the lack of teaching I was given.

And the books were utterly boring.

I've never gotten to read something that I picked out for myself—something I thought I would enjoy.

These two romance books I hold just might be the beginning of a new hobby. Or I'll hate them too, and I can cross reading off my list of things to try for myself.

"We're headed to the first floor. Care to race?" William wiggles his eyebrow at me as we exit the library, him going to the right-handed staircase and me heading toward the one on the left.

"I suppose I could take you up on that challenge. First one to the foyer?"

He nods, his smile lopsided as he takes his stance next to the railing. "Ready?"

"Go!" I yell, taking the stairs two at a time on the way down. William flies down the staircase on his side, but I try to keep my eyes on my own stairs, lest I trip and end this race by breaking my neck.

I huddle the books close to my chest, not holding onto the railing as I move faster and faster down the second staircase. I'm halfway to the foyer, and my adrenaline is so high I don't notice anything else around me.

As I reach the final staircase, I sneak a peek at where William is. He makes eye contact with me as he reaches his final staircase, and it feels like everything in the space between us freezes in time.

He quirks a smile, winking at me. All of a sudden, from one moment to the next, he's jumped up on the staircase railing and is *flying* down it, sliding all the way to the foyer.

I gasp in shock, quickening my feet to catch up with him, but it's no use.

He won.

He laughs as I meet up with him at the bottom, doubled over trying to catch his breath.

I hit him on the shoulder, feigning annoyance. "You cheated!"

"We never specified we had to use our feet the whole way down. I would have slid down all four floors, but I didn't want you to catch on until it was too late."

That makes me laugh, and soon enough, we are

both laughing so hard tears are leaking out of my eyes, making my vision blurry.

So blurry, in fact, that we do not see Kori walk up beside us until he is standing right there, clearing his throat.

I quickly snap to attention, straightening out my outfit and holding the books I took behind my back. I don't know if that's something he'd be upset by, but I'd rather not take the chance.

Truthfully, Kori scares me just a bit.

William is slower to come to, brushing his hair out of his eyes as he relaxes his posture. His eyes are bright from the thrill of our game, his cheeks blooming with color from the rush.

"William," Kori pauses. "A word."

They saunter over to the door in front of the dining hall, far enough away that I can't make out the whole conversation, but still close enough to where I can make out words if I pay attention to their lips.

"...*keep her occupied,*" Kori says, spitting out his words like venom.

"...*not incapable of helping us with...*" William retorts, his jaw muscle ticking in annoyance.

"*Do what you're told,*" Kori bites back, his voice raising so that I can hear his whole statement.

William huffs, retracting himself from the conversation. As he heads back over to me, leaving an angry Kori in his wake, he dawns a smile back on his face as if that conversation didn't happen at all.

Kori takes a deep breath, looking me over. Turning on his heel, he makes his way to the royal hall, slamming the door behind him.

"I apologize for my father's theatrics. He prefers to add flair to the way he does things."

"I've noticed," I smirk, lightening the mood. William offers me his arm and moves us toward the dining room.

My stomach rumbles, reminding me I haven't eaten since lunch with Selene in the garden.

William chuckles. "We can stop and get something on our way."

"I'll be fine to wait if you'd prefer."

"No, I'm hungry too. Winning makes me ravenous." He winks at me, and I laugh, rolling my eyes at him.

William escorts me through the kitchen door instead, nodding hello to everyone we pass. They all light up as he walks by. Clearly, William is beloved here with them.

I'm not sure I could say the same of Kori.

Tarsha walks up to us, gesturing around as if to say, 'what do you need?'.

"Two bowls of soup and bread, please." He responds naturally, as if he's been communicating this way with her his whole life.

Which, I suppose, he has.

We sit at a tall table with barstools while we wait. I place my books next to me, flipping through the pages of the first one to see if anything catches my interest. Tarsha quickly leaves and returns, two steaming bowls of potato soup in her hands.

Covered in cheese, the smell makes my mouth water. Once those are placed in front of us, she makes her way back to grab a crisp loaf of bread straight from the oven and slices it directly before my eyes.

The smell wafts, filling my senses and warming me from the inside out.

I can hardly wait for the soup to cool before taking a large bite with my spoon.

I groan.

This is the best soup I've ever had.

Not that we have much soup in Paralia for me to compare it with.

"Good?" William asks, blowing on his spoon to cool down his own bite.

"I've never had food this good." I pause. "We eat mostly fish in Paralia, accompanied by warmer weather fruits and vegetables. The meals are always light and delectable. You're never quite 'full', but you get used to the feeling."

I wave my hand toward my bowl and the bread, grabbing a slice as I do. "This food feels fulfilling. It makes me feel heavy in the best way. As if I could take a nap right after and it would be the best sleep of my life."

He laughs, nodding along to what I'm saying. "Dip your bread in your soup."

I do, taking a big piece and soaking it up in the potato soup. The bite comes easily, my eyes rolling to the back of my head in delight.

"*This* is the best thing I've ever had," I mumble, my mouth full.

He laughs at me again, the sound fulfilling me from the inside out alongside my meal.

We continue to eat, draining our bowls to the last

drop. I use the last slice of bread to soak up what's left on the bottom of my bowl, eating it quickly so I don't drip anything off it.

A kitchen maid I haven't seen before comes by to collect our dishes and napkins, and William and I are once again on our way. I leave my books in the kitchen, convincing myself I will remember to come back for them later.

Rather than taking me out the kitchen door that connects to the foyer, he holds the door open for me to the dining room.

The table is empty, as is the rest of the room. Taking me past the table, we head to a paneled door in the wall perpendicular to the entrance from the foyer.

William places his hand on the door and it swings open, revealing a grand throne room. Covered in a black flag with silver detailing from top to bottom, the mountainous wall overtakes the far side behind the thrones.

Three thrones sit in the middle of the room as if center stage. The chair's arms and backs look as if they are made from a twisted silver branch, wound up and around to craft the chair's shape.

The cushions are black, contrasting the white the Oresteian royals wear to sit atop its seat.

The biggest throne—Kori's—is on the left. The smallest throne—William's—sits in the middle, and one between those two sizes sits to the right—the Queen's.

There is a glass casing next to the Queen's throne, with the Queen's Crown inside atop a white velvet pillow. Standing directly in front of the case, a guard stands.

I recognize him from my outing with Selene earlier. "Hello again, Haldor."

He nods to me, not moving from his stationary position. The all-black outfit and silver sword strapped on his back makes him look much more intimidating than he did this afternoon handing me a sandwich after a long hour of archery practice.

William gestures toward Haldor, one hand in his pocket. "Haldor, please station yourself outside. I will get you when we are finished."

Again, he nods. Moving toward the door connecting the throne room and the dining room, he makes eye contact with me quickly and the side of his mouth lifts in a smirk.

I scowl at him, unamused.

No one takes me seriously. It boils my blood that he might be thinking I'm a lost cause, or that I'm to blame. For all I know, he's the one that took the Queen's Heart.

I wonder if Haldor even knows it's missing.

It's possible he's the one that took it.

I shake my head, letting go of that thought. What would he have to gain? Probably nothing.

As soon as Haldor has retreated from the room, William opens his arms in surrender.

"Have at it."

I grin in response. "I will."

CHAPTER TWENTY-THREE

I begin by searching the thrones, looking for a trick button, a false lever, or an odd, twisted branch. From there, I move to the flooring, dancing upon the tiles as I see if pressure might swing a hidden door open.

I start to search the walls, running my hands along the stone surface. The coolness of the rock makes me shiver, the storm outside still blowing hard enough that we are on lockdown. If I listen closely, I can hear the whistle of the wind against the mountain.

Nothing comes of my search there either, and I notice William just leaning against the door, staring at me as I work.

"If *you* were a secret passage, where would you hide?" I ask, raising an eyebrow at his smirk.

"I thought you'd never ask." He walks over to the large black flag on the far wall behind the thrones, the silver threading depicting a beautiful picture of Escaeus.

Moving the fabric over, he reveals a small door that my eyes only notice because I am looking for it. It's cut completely into the rock surface, with hardly a seam showing between the wall and the hidden door.

I look at William, curious why he didn't mention this as soon as we walked in.

"I created this."

I snort. "*You* dug out a hole in the middle of this mountain to create a secret passage to… where exactly?"

"That's not what I mean." He pulls back the fabric even more and pushes the door open, sliding itself into the wall, revealing a slim, dark hallway.

"I made this what it is. This was used as a secret passage for the royal family long ago, should rebellion happen while at court. I found it early in my teenage years and tried to mention it to my father, but he waved me off, stating nothing like it existed within our stronghold walls.

"I used to slip away to follow the hall. Filled with dust, webs, and darkness, it took me a few weeks to finally reach the end. And at the end, I found a safe house, tucked away in the rolling mountains covered by peuko trees."

He pauses, as if listening to where Haldor might be on the other side of the door. Lowering his voice, he continues. "The safe house was all but run down to the ground. Forgotten over time, the windows were covered in grime, the furniture stiff when sat upon. I've spent years creating it to be what it is now—my space."

"What does this have to do with the Queen's Heart? I thought that's what we were doing in here?"

"There is no other entrance or exit into this room. The tunnel leads directly to the cottage and that cottage has a front door. It's possible someone found it, used it to travel here, and was able to still make an escape with the jewel. But it would be *very* hard to do unless you were familiar with the layout."

I ponder this. "How did you find the passage in the first place?"

He laughs. "I wanted the flag to be crafted into a cape. Father said no. I tore it off the wall in defiance and loosened the door in the process, which opened just a sliver. I was but twelve or thirteen at the time.

"After I realized what I found, and once father dismissed the idea, I began to dream up the possibility of having my own safe space away from the confines of Escaeus."

"And you're telling me this because you're going to take me, right?"

He looks hesitant.

I huff. "You can't tell me you have a secret cottage without letting me go. What if I find something you may have overlooked?"

He holds his hands up in surrender. "You're right. We can go. It's nearing time to retire for the evening, though, so if you're tired, we can wait until morning."

"I'm not well versed in practicing patience," I say, winking at him as I move to enter the dark tunnel. "Now would be a good time for Selene to show up with her fire fingers."

He laughs, my statement catching him off guard. "Fire fingers?"

"That's what they are!" I exclaim. I follow William

through the tunnel after he shuts the door back behind us. Now completely cocooned in darkness, it's hard to watch where I step.

"I know this tunnel like the back of my hand—hold onto me and I'll lead the way." He finds my arm, linking it with his. The tunnel is barely big enough for us to both squeeze through at the same time, so I end up awkwardly trailing behind.

I relent by letting go of his arm and taking his hand instead, only to find out how cold his fingers are. His pauses for a minute, as if stumbling over his feet. Then, as if he didn't just trip in front of me, he continues on his way.

After minutes of silence, he moves his left hand in my right hand, interlocking our fingers. My heart is beating out of my chest as his thumb brushes the back of my hand.

Still leading the way, our position feels so much more intimate than it did a minute ago. While I've touched his hand, we've never held hands like this.

And I don't mind the feeling of his hand in mine at all.

The thought scares me, knowing what that could mean for both of us—for me.

I'm not here permanently.

And Callious is waiting for me back home.

Refusing to lessen my grip, I keep up with William's long strides as we continue on. My eyes have started to adjust to the tunnel's walls, and he was right—it is dusty back here.

I sneeze involuntarily, dust making its way into my nose.

Sheepishly he says, "It's been a while since I've been through here. The dust somehow always comes back when I'm away."

All of a sudden, it feels as though the ground is shaking beneath my feet. The rumble intensifies, a trembling resonating within my bones. The air fills with a chilling sensation.

I fall into William, a roaring sound filling my ears. The tunnel quakes, making me uneasy.

"What is that?" I say, clinging onto his arm for dear life. The shift is disorienting, throwing me off balance.

And just as quickly as it started, it stops.

William straightens me, helping me regain my footing. "Oh, that must have been the dragons."

My jaw drops as I whirl to completely face him again. "You have dragons?"

He smirks. "No, if we had dragons, you would have seen them by now."

I hit him on the arm and force a laugh, my heart still beating wildly. His distraction worked, though—I feel like I can stand on my own again.

"That must have been an avalanche. When the storm is bad enough like it was predicted to be tonight, snow will roll off Escaeus in piles, creating that sound, making the mountain feel as if it's splitting apart."

He looks at me pointedly. "I suppose your father may never forgive me if the mountain were to come down on you."

I exhale sharply. "That would be a hard one to explain, that's true."

He smiles at my sarcasm, takes my hand once

more, and continues to lead us on our way through the hidden passage.

▲▲▲

After what feels like an eternity, we make our way to a closed off wall at the end of the tunnel. Rather than opening it into a door like the other side, William lets go of my hand and pushes up on the ceiling on top of us.

My hand mourns his own as I watch him open a trap door within the ceiling. Dim light floods through the opening, causing me to look away while my eyes readjust. Just hardly taller than we are, William jumps and grabs the ledge, hoisting himself up onto the floor of the cottage.

He reaches down to grab my arms, instructing me to use the wall to climb up. Painstakingly, I make my way, finally sitting on the floor of the cottage.

I attempt to catch my breath as I take in my surroundings. William walks to the corner of the room and lights a lantern standing on a small table.

"Penelope, this is the Eremos cottage—my isolated place."

CHAPTER TWENTY-FOUR

The Eremos Cottage might be the most beautiful thing I've ever seen.

It's simple—just four walls surrounding all the rooms you could need. The flooring is cold beneath my hands, the wood paneling rough with age.

The trap door leads to the living room, if you can call it that. Floor to ceiling windows overlook the dark, snowy exterior, the storm blowing on.

I can just barely see snow-capped peuko trees surrounding the cottage, covering it from the view of those who may stumble upon it.

The living room holds a dark gray leather couch, and a wood burning heater in the corner. Piles of white blankets and pillows are thrown about haphazardly, making it feel warm and inviting.

In the corner, there's a small piano. Dried flowers in a vase sit on top, along with a candle with a half-burned wick.

This piano is nothing like the one in the stronghold.

That piano is a white gleam—like fresh snow. This one is dark and muddy—like messy, sandy shores. The bench's leather seat is cracked and old, the piano's wood dry and warped.

There's a small kitchen joined to the living room. The lantern's light bleeds into this space, nothing separating the two rooms but the couch. A stove and basin are all that abound in these rooms, with a few baskets and shelving options to store whatever dry goods you might hold here in case the worst happens.

I get up, walking toward a small wall that separates the living room from the bedroom. There is no door connecting the two, just open space free to walk through.

The bed is large, taking up most of the bedroom. A white quilt, down-filled and in a pile, sits atop the bed —as if someone woke with a start and didn't have time to make it before leaving to be on their way.

The bed's pillows lean next to another massive window along one wall, with a large bookshelf standing along the adjacent wall.

I run my finger along the spines of the books sitting on the shelves, worn and rough with use. I don't recognize any of the titles, but I dream of taking a book or two from what must be William's personal hoard so I might try to enjoy them as well.

There's a door shut in the corner of the bedroom, presumably for a washroom or toilet.

The wind outside finally lets up, and I can see snow falling in the now gentle breeze, even though it has long since turned dark outside.

While I wander, I can hear William lighting the

wood heater in the living room, and the space instantly feels homier and cozier.

My eyes grow tired, having hardly noticed just how exhausted I am from all I've done today.

I walk back into the living room to sit on the couch, covering my cold body with one of the heavy blankets. The soft material begs me to fall asleep right here, to forget about the rest of the world right now.

I fight my body trying to lay down, keeping my eyes on William and the fire now blazing in the heater.

"It's gorgeous here. How do you convince yourself to go back?"

He laughs, forsaking the fire to come sit next to me, grabbing his own blanket on the way.

William faces the fire, rather than facing me, and I feel cold in the absence of his gaze. The firelight dances among his sharp features, drawing my eyes to his face.

"It's hard to go back," he admits, still staring into the fire's glow. "I find myself having to come up with excuses as to why I shouldn't come back here, because I know as soon as I am, I'd rather not be anywhere else."

I nod, understanding. That's what the Neronian Sea is to me—my isolated escape.

Of course, how isolated can a place be when you share it with a friend?

My head nods in exhaustion, and William whips his eyes to meet mine. "Are you that tired? We can go back." He jumps off the couch, extending a hand to mine.

I snuggle into the couch further, protesting. "It's

just so… inviting here. I feel reluctant to leave, if I'm honest."

He hesitates, his hand still outstretched. "We can stay here for the night, if you'd like. I'm happy to take the couch. There's a washroom attached to the bedroom, and the water runs hot here."

"Won't you get in trouble if you're needed at the stronghold but not around?"

He chuckles, finally relenting and sitting back down on the couch. I extend my blanket to him, and he takes half of it, our legs touching beneath.

"No one there will even notice I'm gone. If anything, if father goes looking for me, he will assume I'm out 'keeping you busy'." He quotes those last words with his fingers, giving me a half-hearted smile with it.

I laugh. "I suppose I could go for a hot shower, then."

"Be my guest, Penelope. This cottage is now yours just as much as it is mine."

▲▲▲

My shower might be the best shower I've ever taken. William wasn't kidding when he said the water runs *hot*. I scrub with the soap he has on hand, making me smell like he does—a scent of cinnamon and vanilla.

After toweling off, I realize I don't have another set of clothes to wear. Within the small bathroom, there's a tall dresser tucked away in the corner. I begin opening drawers, finding a pair of white pants I can cinch at the waist so they don't fall off. The shirt I find is big and long, most likely William's size.

I hope he doesn't mind me taking his clothes.

I leave the towel hanging on a hook on the back of the door and grab my old outfit, placing them in the corner of the bedroom so I remember to take them with me tomorrow.

My wet hair drips down my back, and I take my hair tie from earlier and begin to braid it as I walk back to the living room.

William sees me enter, gesturing for me to sit at his feet. "Let me braid it for you."

I pause. "You know how to braid?"

He snorts as I move to the floor in front of him, leaning against the couch. "Selene made me learn. She said it would come in handy someday."

"I suppose she was right."

He hesitantly moves his hands to grab my hair, slowly and carefully combing through my curls with his fingers.

The crackle of the fire is the only sound as he gently braids my hair. I can feel the water dripping down my back, and I remember I'm wearing his clothes.

"I hope you don't mind me borrowing your items. I didn't bring anything other than what I was wearing today."

"My clothes look good on you," he responds, finishing the braid. He motions with his hand, asking for my hair tie off my wrist. I remove it, handing it to him.

After tying back my hair, he places his hands on my

shoulder gently, and I look over my right shoulder at him. The firelight reflects off his ice-blue eyes, drawing me in.

My eyelids droop, and he takes note of the tiredness on my face.

Smiling softly, he pats my arm. "I think it's time for you to sleep."

I nod, disappointed. I wish I had the energy to stay up, to talk. Hiding away in the Eremos cottage with him sounds like the perfect way to spend a snowed-in evening.

He helps me up, scooting around on the couch to stand and offer me a hand. I take it, pulling myself up with his assistance. His presence is intoxicating, making me unsteady where I stand.

With one last long look at each other, I make my way to the bedroom, and he lays back down on the couch.

I sigh, laying back on the most comfortable mattress I've ever felt, guaranteeing this might be the best night's sleep I've ever had.

CHAPTER TWENTY-FIVE

THE MORNING COMES QUICKLY, A FOGGY LIGHT trailing in through the tall windows. The air is cold, but the storm seems to have passed. If anything, this is the clearest I've ever seen the weather look here in the few days since I arrived.

William claims it's just after dawn, and we make our way back to the stronghold through the tunnel we came in from, sealing back the trap door and throne room door completely.

When we exit the throne room, Haldor is still standing watch on the other side of that door. Him and William nod to each other, with Haldor re- entering to take up his post inside.

I part with William and make my way to my bedroom to change, falling back into a lighter sleep once I lay upon my bed. My body is sore, and while I slept deeply last night, I feel as though I'm still dragging.

▲▲▲

Days go by with a similar routine to that. I'm hounded with random questions by William at breakfast, Selene and I practice archery until my arms feel as though they're going to fall off long into the afternoons, and I spend time in the library with William researching the tree's existence and the Heart's disappearance, to no avail.

One morning early on, William surprises me with dried flowers from their city's market to place in the empty vases in my room.

Handing them to me from behind his back, he says, "I wanted to be a part of the small group that has given you a gift firsthand, rather than something someone else had the chance to love first."

Gushing over the dry colors, they are the first thing I set my eyes on every morning. Though that is the first gift he's given me, and one that will likely last forever, it does not feel as though it will be the last.

A few of my evenings are spent by the fire of the Eremos Cottage, speaking about anything and everything. William is so easy to chat with, and the cottage is the most serene space. I feel honored he would share this delightful place with me.

For the first time, I'm a partaker in someone else's secret knowledge rather than being in the background and unneeded. It's a welcome change—one I wouldn't have expected from coming here.

Before I know it, two weeks have passed. As time goes along, William's presence is becoming scarcer and harder to grasp. His father has demanded more of his time, requesting answers and help in the war looming just over the horizon.

I find myself finally writing to my father, letting him into a touch of the knowledge I have received. I feel hesitant to give him all I know, lest he use it against Kori, or Oresteia as a whole.

Despite my trying not to, I have grown attached to this Kingdom and land. I have become especially partial to a few of the people within it, in spite of Kori's cold existence.

Selene and I take frequent walks around the stronghold, finally showing me most rooms within. I'm allowed to visit the stables outside the stronghold, and I sneak Agrius treats and pets as often as I'm able.

One evening before bed, I'm back in the throne room, retracing steps and smoothing over stones along the wall, trying to find what I'm missing.

Haldor is once again stationed outside the throne room, accepting my request for privacy. I feel so defeated—unsure of what I can do to help William in this search. I mark where the crown is again, looking at it closely.

All of a sudden, the sound of stone scraping against stone startles me and I whip toward the screech. The flag in front of the tunnel moves, and I breathe a sigh of relief. William must be coming back from Eremos.

This morning, he was absent from both breakfast and the library, so I've tried to distract myself from his sudden disappearance. He did not write to tell me where he was, so I assumed all day that he was busy with meetings with Kori.

"You startled me," I say, a hand on my beating heart. I walk toward the flag, beginning to grab the corner to get it out of his way.

And I find myself face to face with Callious.

I gape.

He stares.

We both stand there, frozen.

"I..." I begin, my words stuck in a lump in my throat.

"Pen!" He cries, wrapping me in his arms, his head atop mine. "I was so worried I wouldn't be able to find you."

I suffocate in his embrace. "How are you here? I've been waiting for you to write!" I release myself from his clutch and move backwards. I'm still stunned, unsure of what to say.

"I got your letter. This was the soonest I could come. I couldn't write all I wanted to, it had to be done in person..." His words bleed together, frantic and rushed.

I cut him off, clutching his arm. "We can't talk here." I sneak a peek back at the door, remembering Haldor outside. Even though I could, I don't want to take Callious to the Eremos cottage. It just feels... wrong.

"We can talk in my room. Close the tunnel back, and I'll take care of the guard outside." I leave him to it, moving to open the door a crack.

"Haldor," I start. He grunts his reply, looking at me over his shoulder. If he notices my nervous demeanor, he doesn't let it show. "Could I ask you to send for William? I'm aware he is busy, but whenever he's able, I'd like to speak with him in my room."

He nods, turning on his heel at once to head to the kitchen. Just like that, the dining room is now empty.

Now all I have to do is get Callious from the throne room to my bedroom.

Easier said than done.

By now, he's finished with the tunnel entrance and is beginning to peek out the throne room door.

How subtle of him.

I motion for him to follow me and to be extremely quiet.

We creep out of the dining hall and make a hard left to the royal hall. The doorknob glows as I place my hand on it, and the door swings wide open.

Callious is able to follow me into the hall with ease. Thank the sun no one else is currently out and about.

I feel uncertain regarding whether or not he will be able to enter my room, and whether or not I want him to have permission to.

I suppose I have to if I don't want him to get caught.

We reach my room, and I walk through the door frame with no hesitation like always.

Callious tries to follow, but an invisible barrier knocks him back. He looks at me, bewildered.

Unsure of how this works, I say a bit quietly, "Callious, you may enter my room."

He falls through the barrier, barely catching himself as the room allows him entry.

"What was that?" He exclaims, checking himself

from head to toe in astonishment. "How did it do that?"

I shut the door, moving to gesture that we can sit on my bed. I watch him take in his surroundings as he does, noticing my blanket I brought from home, the dagger in its sheath on my pillow.

I still haven't convinced Selene to practice throwing it with me, and William has been too busy.

Finally, his eyes make their way to my neck, where the necklace he gave me still sits along my collarbone.

Suddenly, I feel bare under his penetrating gaze.

What is he doing here? What am I to say to him? It's never felt this awkward between us in the seventeen years of friendship we have, but I find myself at a complete loss for words.

"Why are you here, Callious?" I ask, sitting beside him on my bed.

He runs his hand along the quilt. "I had to come, P. I got your letter, and I couldn't write back. Not in a way that would make sense. I needed to come here, to see you. To understand what was going on."

He pauses for a breath before continuing, "The war is coming. It's practically *there*. I've risen in rank—I'm a Captain. Can you believe that? *Me!*"

He looks frantically around the room, gesturing wildly with his hands. "I took leave to come here—I trekked across the Stenos Isthmus by myself to come find you. You're not safe here with war on the horizon. I snuck through Oresteia's gate and found my way to that little house…"

"The Eremos cottage." I cut in, unable to help

myself. I find myself growing frustrated at his monologue, wishing he'd get to the point.

"The what?" He asks. I shrug and shake my head, not willing to give him more information.

"I only had a map with bare bones—I had no idea that tunnel would lead me here. But I am so glad it did. I didn't think I'd be able to find you in time…"

"*Why* are you *here*, Callious?" I interrupt, no longer able to take his ramblings.

"What does it look like, Nelly?" His green eyes blink back at me, obviously confused. "I'm here to take you back to Paralia. I'm here to save you."

CHAPTER TWENTY-SIX

I STAND, DUMBFOUNDED.

Save me?

What in the sun's name gave him that idea?

I pinch the skin between my eyes in frustration. "Callious, I don't need saving. I'm doing just fine here!"

He stares at me. "You said you missed me."

I wave my arms, exasperated. "Of course I missed you! I was gone for one day and we had hardly been apart longer than that in the past. But instead of writing back to me, you chose to travel all this way to return me to Paralia?"

"The sun guided me here! What else was I supposed to do—wait for a letter to be delivered and then wait for your response back?"

"What do you mean the sun guided you *here*? Does my family know you came?"

He swallows, ducking his eyes from me. "I had to tell your father so that I could get his seal for my journey across the Isthmus and through the gates. Otherwise, our army wouldn't have let me leave."

He pauses, earnest with his tone. "The sun rose directly behind the gate the morning I received your letter while I was doing rounds with our guards. It's typically more to the right. I had never seen that before—it felt as though it was calling me here to you."

"First of all, that's a bit ridiculous." I begin fuming, unable to contain my anger at this declaration. "And you *told* my *father?* After I asked you not to? I just wrote to him for the first time a few days ago!"

Callious blushes, running his hand through the back of his hair. "He wasn't extremely... pleased... that you wrote me first."

I snort. "I could have told you that."

Shaking my head, I begin to pace the length of my room, leaving Callious still sitting on my bed.

"What have you learned on Paralia's side? Surely you would not forsake that part of my message in asking what you know?" I pause. "Or have you forgotten that I needed your help with *that* matter?"

He wrings his hands together. "The war is so much bigger than what we thought before you left. We are stationed in Komeus right now, barely keeping our ranks tight enough to ward off unrest. The city is unruly." Callious pauses, looking at me. "The army is itching for a fight. I can hardly keep my company in line."

"What does that have to do with what was taken?"

"They *want* to go to battle, Nel. If it was one of the Frey that took it, it was so we could finally hash out all the tension that has gathered within our Kingdom for the last twelve years."

I look at him quizzically, frantically putting together some pieces within my mind. "Did you take it?"

He blinks. "What?"

I spit out my words. "You heard me, Callious. Did. You. Take. It."

He shakes his head, ever so slightly. "You can't mean what was stolen?" He pauses, throwing his hands up. "I didn't even know it was a jewel that was taken!"

I stare, not relenting, my arms crossing of their own volition. "I didn't tell you it was a jewel—only that an important artifact was stolen." Pausing, I let him sit within our own tension—this battle being waged between the two of us. "What have you heard on Paralia's shores, *Callious*?"

"Tell me why you need to know so badly, *Penelope*." He spits out my full name like venom.

I draw back, stunned. I can't remember the last time he has called me by my given name.

Under normal circumstances, I would have been thrilled by that.

I throw my hands in the air. "The fate of our Kingdoms depends upon it! It could mean we are erased from existence. That our Kingdoms would collapse."

"That's not a good enough answer." He rises from where he was sitting on my bed. "I'm going to war over this cause. I'm in charge of men who might lose their *lives*. What is going on and what are you doing to stop it?"

"Is that what this is about? That I told you I

couldn't go with you to fight?" I huff. "Once again you believe running is my only option."

"No, you made it *very* clear that you would not run from this opportunity."

I roll my eyes at his sarcasm. "I'm doing everything I can!"

"It's not enough!" He yells, color blooming on his face in anger.

I square my gaze with his, a fire lighting within me.

"It's never enough for *anyone*. Not my family, not the Kingdom—and you know that. You've sat and empathized with me. You've taken time to listen to my frustrations and affirm me."

My words feel stuck in my throat, frustration rising from within me. "I never thought the day would come that I wouldn't be enough for *you*."

Callious looks as if I slapped him. Which, in a way, I did.

We've never said such words to each other.

There's a knock at my door, lazy and unhurried. I look at Callious, and he raises an eyebrow at me. I don't like how we are leaving things, but I can't help but be curious at who could need me right now.

And I wonder how long they've been standing there.

And what they heard.

Suns above, please let these rooms be enchantingly soundproof.

I wave for Callious to hide in my bathroom, and to be quiet.

I go to open the door and find William leaning

against the frame on the other side. He looks tired, unkempt. I've never seen him look quite so unrested.

"I heard you needed me?" He winks, kicking himself away from where he leans to stand fully in front of me.

I hesitate, unsure of what to do. William notices my hesitation, his eyebrows furrowing.

"Hey, is everything okay? I'm sorry I couldn't come sooner—my father has had me tied up in war council all day." He reaches to place his hand on my chin to lift my eyes, but the invisible barrier that is my door stops him.

He brings his hand back, having forgotten that he hasn't had permission to enter my room. Though, he hasn't needed permission until now. We've not had a reason to establish that boundary yet.

Suddenly, footsteps sound behind me, and I see William's eyes grow wide as he takes in my secret guest. His jaw contracts, a muscle ticking in apprehension.

"And who," he asks me. "Is this?"

CHAPTER TWENTY-SEVEN

I QUICKLY DEBATE WITHIN MY MIND THE PROS AND CONS of denying I know who Callious is and why he's here. It might be easy to dismiss the real reason he came all this way.

I could potentially blame the sadness behind the distance, or maybe that he had a letter that needed to be delivered to me personally, urgently.

Except, I don't know how long he was there and how much he heard, if anything.

Unfortunately, William is too smart for anything I might try to pull.

And it would eat me alive to lie to him.

That, and Callious feels the need to talk before I'm able to try to mutter a single word.

"Who are you?" Callious asks with caution, an eyebrow raised at William's appearance. With how rumpled William is, it's easy to see how he might be viewed as someone who is not the Oresteian prince.

William leans against my door frame once more,

still not permitted to enter, a picture of cool arrogance. He's trying to appear unbothered, but his unease at the situation comes off of him in waves.

Soft, muddied, yellow waves.

I stare at him, blinking, trying to rid the color from my mind, but the color persists in bleeding off his person.

Whipping my head to Callious, I find a dark shade of blue radiating from him, seriousness emitting from his tone and body language.

I look down at my own arms, my own body, trying to see if I might have an aura of color portrayed to the world around me as well.

My skin looks ashen—gray almost.

William must notice my uncertainty, because he softly asks, "What is it?"

"Can you see that?" I respond, a jittery nervousness taking over my reaction.

He shakes his head at me, confusion lining his features. Meanwhile, Callious still stands in my room, looking at us back and forth.

Realization dawns on him, his jaw now tightly shut. "You must be the prince whose time is constantly being stolen." He pauses, tapping his chin. "What was your name again… Wilbert, right?"

I roll my eyes, but William looks at Callious with amusement.

It appears he's willing to play this little game.

"So I am. And *you* must be the best friend who once yelled at Penelope to be more careful, though she had hardly done anything wrong. I do believe I recall your name… it's on the tip of my tongue." William kicks himself off the door frame, standing firm on his two feet. "Charles?"

They engage in a stand-off, staring down their opponent. Pride and something else begin to flood my senses… jealousy, maybe? Vibrant purples and greens flow between them, livening up the space. Their colors clash together before my eyes, dancing in the air between.

Surely that can't be right.

Not wanting to watch this go on for much longer, I address Callious first.

"Quit it," I say, looking from one to the other. "Both of you, please."

After what feels like minutes, William breaks eye contact first, moving his gaze from Callious' to mine with a bashful smile playing on his lips.

Good—he should be embarrassed.

"William, would you like permission to enter my room?"

"I thought you'd never ask." He winks, and I feel my cheeks grow hot.

"You may enter." I wave him in, now moving to go sit on my bed. I feel like leaving to shower, to give them space to figure out whatever is happening between the two of them.

This is too much for me right now.

William extends a hand to Callious, marching right up to him with purpose. "William," he says.

Callious looks at him with unease, but finally reaches out his own hand, shaking William's. "Callious," he responds.

William smiles, dropping the handshake. "I know." Addressing me, he turns. "Start at the beginning."

I relay the story to William as best as I can without giving away the fact that Callious found the Eremos cottage, our fight, and the tension that was between us before William showed up and knocked on my door.

Though he probably already knows.

I also decide to leave out the parts that might make Callious look especially bad, despite the fact that I'm incredibly angry with him and desperately wish for someone to be on my side.

Even though I'm upset, I don't want to turn William against my longest and closest friend the first moment they meet.

As I finish, William says to Callious, "You didn't have to sneak in. You could have asked for leave to see Penelope specifically."

He blushes, looking down and kicking at the stone floor. "To be transparent, I had assumed she wasn't being kept somewhere that was visitable. I didn't want Kori to breathe down King Zannan's neck during my presence here."

William blinks, appalled. "You thought we were keeping her prisoner?"

Callious corrects him. "I thought you *could* be. You have to realize she found out one night in advance that she was leaving, and we had no information regarding what was truly going on. It felt too sticky to leave in the hands of someone else."

He now looks at me, apologetically. "Especially once I received your letter, P."

"What letter?" William asks, interrupting Callious' silent apology.

I go to respond, but Callious cuts in first. "I have it." He reaches into the pocket of his trousers, and I just now take the time to register his all-black attire that he's wearing.

He looks like one of Oresteia's guards.

I wonder if that was on purpose.

Callious hands William the note, and I grow nervous again.

What if something I said is incriminating?

What if I accidentally betrayed William's trust in me by writing what I did to Callious?

I try to think back on what I said, but I can hardly recall the words I wrote all those weeks ago. It feels like it's been a year that I've been here—that I'm a completely different person than when I first showed up.

William quickly reads the letter, nodding along as his eyes skim over the words on the crinkled, worn page.

He smiles, looking at me. "My father does require a lot of my time, you're right."

I grin back, the ice broken between us. I hadn't realized how worried I was that he would be upset until his eyes shined in my direction.

Callious clears his throat, and I duck my head. I had forgotten he was here too.

"Penelope, may I have a private word?"

Surprised, I nod. I follow William into the wash-room, waiting for him to start.

"How mad are you?" He asks me in a whisper, keeping his voice low.

I murmur back, "How much did you hear?"

His face drops, sadness within his eyes. "I heard enough. The timing of my knock was intentional, unfortunately."

He pauses, thinking. "I was going to leave, but my curiosity got the better of me. The raised voices made me worry that you were in trouble or hurt. I'm sorry if I betrayed your trust in that way." He reaches up, tucking a piece of hair behind my ear.

As he takes his hand away, he allows it to caress the side of my face ever so gently. The skin of his hand is cool and soft, and I can't help but close my eyes and lean into his touch.

"I can make him leave," he says, still holding onto me. "You don't have to finish this right now."

A tear slips from my right eye, but William's thumb catches it and wipes it away before it can fall too far. I nod, not being able to voice my wants out loud.

I am so overwhelmed.

I peel my eyes open, looking up into his. I am hit by the care and understanding I see there and realize just how wrong I've been.

Things with Callious will never be able to stay the same, because I am no longer the same.

But William has consistently met me where I'm at and helped me become just who I want to be in the short time I've been here.

He sees me, and there is an intimacy there that I want to explore. I will never again be this person that I am right now, and I no longer want to stand by and wish this time away.

I want to slow down and be with him, rather than waiting to see what might happen.

Away from Paralia's shores, Callious' influence, and my family's prying eyes, I finally feel like *me.*

And I've come to find that I really like who I am without them around.

And I really like it here.

I sigh, a confession at the tip of my tongue. Instead, a question slips from my mouth. "Tomorrow, could you teach me how to throw a dagger?"

He smiles, removing his hand from my cheek to tenderly hold the hand at my side. "I would be honored to show you."

We exit the washroom, only to find Selene now standing on the other side of my open-door, conversing with Callious excitingly, an aura of light pink glowing from her figure.

I mentally smack myself in the forehead, unbelieving that we left my door wide open.

The only way this could get more chaotic is if Kori showed up.

Suns above, please do not let that happen.

"Callious, you and I are going to leave to discuss what's going to happen next." He looks at Selene, then at me. "I trust you both will have a restful night. I will fill you in at breakfast."

Selene blushes, ducking her head from my eye contact and takes her leave without another word, slipping into her bedroom quietly.

Callious trails behind William, following him to

wherever he has in mind. I hesitate, questioning whether I should say something else in regard to our previous fight.

Before I can, Callious beats me to it.

Peering at me intently over his shoulder, he calls my name.

"Pen," he says, defeated. "You will always be enough for me."

And without another word, he's gone, the door shutting tight behind him.

CHAPTER TWENTY-EIGHT

The next morning after breakfast, William and I take a walk to the garden where Selene and I have been practicing archery. The three of us sat in silence in the dining room after William told us Callious would be staying for a few days, and that Selene's task would be to keep him out of Kori's eyes.

I'm still figuring out what I'd like to do with him.

Right now, nothing.

As we walk, William asks, "So... 'Nel', huh?" I huff. Of course he heard one of my many awful nicknames during Callious and I's fight yesterday.

"Nel, Nelly, Pen, P. If you can think of it, I've probably been called it. Callious especially prefers to use short names to refer to me, but my siblings do as well." I debate whether to go on. "Do you have any nicknames?" I ask.

"I am not permitted to be called anything other than my given name. Father believes there is power in calling someone by their full name. By allowing others to call me something else, it deems me a weak-willed person."

I consider this. "And what is your stance?"

He smiles, reaching to brush a hand across my cheek.

"I believe there is nothing more special than loving and trusting someone enough to allow them to choose a name for you that represents who you are to them."

"My family and Callious have only ever used nick-names for myself. Even when I was introduced to your father, my name was shortened. It is very rare my full name is what comes out of their mouths. To be honest, I've grown tired of it."

He smiles a coy smile at me, dropping his hand. "Do you like hearing your name on my tongue?"

I grin back, enjoying this flirty game we play. "I like my name on your lips most of all."

"Then 'Penelope' is it, from now until when the stars claim me."

"And for you, William? What name do you prefer on my lips?"

"If you will have it, I'd like you to have the honor of being the only one in my life to call me something other than my birth name. I don't care what you call me, so long as it's what you decide."

"Will," I say resolutely.

"Will?"

I grab his hand as we walk, interlocking our fingers. "Yes, that's what I'd like to call you."

He chuckles and we continue, swinging our hands together as if we walk like this constantly—a feeling I could easily get used to.

Looking up to the cloud-filled afternoon sky, he whispers to himself, "Will."

▲▲▲

Finally, we reach the garden. Haldor has been trailing behind us a ways away—much further than he did when it was just me and Selene. Sitting on the fallen log, William begins to show me a series of stretches to go through to warm up my body before we begin throwing.

Selene and I did not stretch before we practiced, and my body paid the price.

"You've got me wondering now, with all our talk of names. What does your name mean?" He pauses briefly. "If you don't mind me asking."

"Is that your question for today?"

He smiles at me, blue eyes lighting up. "If you'll allow it to be."

I nod. "It means 'weaver'. Being the youngest, I suppose my parents believed that I would be one to weave our family's fate together as the final heir." Snorting, I continue, "I don't know what gave them that idea, though."

"My name means 'protector'." Now it's his turn to snort, kicking snow as he walks. "As if my father would ever let me be the one to 'protect' anything." He quotes that word with his fingers, his tone dripping in sarcasm.

"You may not be allowed to 'protect'," I motion with my fingers, "But I am glad you're allowed to teach. I've been wanting to learn how to throw my dagger with precision ever since Selene used it to get me out here."

He gives me a questioning look and I frown. "She refused to show me. She said only you would be willing to do that."

At this, he laughs so hard he doubles over. "She used dagger lessons as a way to bribe you out here?"

I nod, laughing along with him. Now that I know Selene, I realize just how foolish I was to believe she would be someone who could teach me.

Not that she would be bad at it, but she is just *so* very good at archery.

"That might be the best thing I've ever heard. I cannot wait to not let her hear the end of that."

We finish our stretches and Haldor leaves to check the perimeter, leaving William and I alone. He walks to the targets to move them closer.

"Selene will complain once she sees I've moved these and realizes she will have to put them back herself."

"I'm sure Haldor would do it for her," I say, not realizing how that comment might sound. "I didn't mean he likes her, or anything. I just meant he's very kind."

William brushes his hands through his hair, knocking off the snow that's fallen onto it from our trek through the trees. "I know what you mean. She's not interested in Haldor anyway." He pauses. "If I'm not speaking out of turn, it did appear that Callious might have caught her eye."

He eyes me from where he is next to me, as if gauging my reaction.

I reach up and touch my necklace. "I noticed that too." I gasp, mind going a mile a minute. "That reminds me—I saw their colors!"

William—Will, I mean—looks at me quizzically. "Their... colors?"

"Yours too! It was as if their emotions were on display in an aura surrounding their person. I *saw* what they were feeling."

Not giving him the chance to cut in, I keep going. "Do you remember how you said I might have magic? What if that's what this is?"

"When did you first notice it?"

I think back to yesterday's events, recalling what happened after Callious and I fought.

"It began after I was angry—angrier than I've ever been, truthfully." I breathe. "Especially at Callious. I opened the door, and you were leaning there. What were you feeling right then?"

He considers, thinking back to last night's happenings. "I felt uneasy—I wasn't sure what exactly I'd be walking into. I didn't know if you were okay."

I nod, my assumption from yesterday correct. "Your aura was muddy yellow. It came off of you in waves, much like it did for Callious and Selene too. I even looked down at myself, and I was gray. Did I look gray to you last night?"

He shakes his head. "If anything, you looked red with anger and frustration. Maybe even on the brink of tears."

I ignore that comment and look at him excitedly. "Could it be true? Could I have magic?" I ramble on. "How did your magic first come about?"

He laughs, patting the log for me to scoot closer. "My father attempted to have a tutor teach me piano. I was so frustrated at how hard it was to follow along when this teacher obviously knew nothing. I screamed at him, begging him to let me do it myself."

He waits before continuing on. "My father came in and asked the teacher to leave. Once he was gone, father began yelling back at me, saying he was only doing this for my benefit. I hit my hands on the keys, playing a note that would truly make a wolf howl. An illusion of a jagged cliff's edge jumped in front of our eyes, scaring us both nearly to death."

"Would anger be a trigger, then?" I ask.

He nods. "Whatever happened, we will figure it out together." Will stands, extending a hand to me. "Much like teaching you to throw your dagger."

Clasping his hand, I rise.

CHAPTER TWENTY-NINE

W‌ILL GOES OVER BASIC FOOTWORK WITH ME, HELPING me practice my balance and stance.

"This is much different than shooting an arrow. The dagger must become an extension of your arm, the line straight and narrow."

He demonstrates, taking his own dagger out of its sheath on his side.

It stands out against the bright white snow of our surroundings, the metal a sharp onyx color to match the Kingdom's guard's weapons.

The tip is sharp, delicately pointed at the top. His handle has the emblem of Escaeus on the front in silver, the rest of the hilt a stark black.

"Your dagger is gorgeous," I exhale, my embarrassment at my own dagger making my cheeks red. "Where did you get it?"

"I crafted it myself in the city," he pauses. "You haven't been to Copolis for an evening yet, have you?"

I shake my head.

He grins, obviously delighted at that answer. "We will have to change that, should the weather hold."

I attempt to move in his likeness, mimicking his stance and throw. I keep falling over, clumsily unable to keep my stance solid.

"Let me help." He throws his dagger at a nearby tree, hardly looking in that direction as he does it. The dagger hits the tree in the middle, hitting the tree with a solid *thunk.*

I huff as he moves behind me, annoyance taking over. He softly grabs my arms in his hands and kicks my feet to be just a bit wider than they are.

Slowly, he pulls me through the moves he's been showing me for the last hour. Straightening my spine, I hoist my arm up with his help and shift my shoulder to point to the closest target.

I can feel his warm breath on the back of my neck —his presence is *extremely* distracting.

Goosebumps cover my arms beneath my layers, and I thank the sun that the weather requires sleeves, so he can't see what exactly he's doing to me.

What he's always done to me.

We practice the throw, not releasing my dagger just yet.

"That one was good! Try on your own. I'll be right here." Will steps aside, going to the tree to get back his own dagger with a smooth retrieval.

He crosses his arms, now leaning on the tree. Cocking an eyebrow at me, he waits.

I turn my attention back to the target not more than ten feet in front of me and run through the steps on my own.

Finally, I extend my arm and release the dagger, making sure to focus my power on my arm and not just in my hand or wrist.

My dagger releases from my grasp and flies through the air—directly to the right of the target. It hits the soft snow underneath it, burrowing itself immediately.

Sheepishly, I look at Will. "At least it was the right distance?"

He kicks himself off the tree, going to retrieve my dagger. "Your aim could use a little work, that's true."

I laugh as I take it back from him. Our gloved hands graze as he hands it over, and chills go down my spine. "You're good at everything right away. How do you do it?"

"Years of practice, boredom, and loneliness have allowed me to perfect my craft. Do you really think my father would let his lone heir not be able to wield a sword or throw a dagger?"

"I forgot just how differently our upbringing was for a second. I'm sorry."

He clasps me on the shoulder. "No need to apologize—I understand that you weren't given the same chances as many others. You're not going to get it on your first try. That's what practice is for."

He looks at me up and down as a smile blooms on his wind-stricken face. "Plus, it sounds like you weren't doing *that* bad at archery. Perhaps you'd rather perfect that craft?"

I laugh, my head tipped back in joy. "Who told you that? Surely Selene's not the type to lie."

"Oh, you'd be surprised at the secrets she's able to

keep." He hits his shoulder against mine, gesturing that I should try again.

I do, once more making the same mistake except this time to the left. Will leaves to retrieve my dagger again from the deep snow of the garden.

"I want to be able to fight and protect myself. I want to feel as though this gift I was given so long ago wasn't just so I could have something pretty to carry around." I stomp, my frustration enveloping my tone. "I want to be useful in this upcoming war."

"Do you plan on fighting against me? Because if so, I'd prefer you miss your target." His sarcasm makes me smile, even though I am reluctant to do so.

"Keep trying, Penelope. You've only just begun."

▲▲▲

Hundreds of throws and many, *many* hours later, I've not yet hit the target once.

My patience is thin, my stomach is hungry, and my arms are tired.

"I'm sorry I'm taking up so much of your time and patience," I say, my eyes downcast. "We can go whenever you wish."

"Hey," Will gets to me in three strides, taking my chin and lifting it so I meet his eyes. "Why are you insecure about where your feet stand? The mountains do not apologize for taking up space, and neither should you. Try again."

I nod, determination filling my veins. I right my stance, telling myself this is my last attempt for today.

Nothing good comes without rest, and if I keep throwing, I'm going to burn myself out before even getting to truly start.

I plant my feet in the snow, making sure to stand straight with confidence in the power I have behind my throw.

I lift my chin, a slight chilly breeze now running through my curls from my left.

I use my left hand to point at the target, bringing my right arm back behind me, loosely holding my dagger's hilt in my grasp.

I breathe in slowly, letting the mountain air remind me that I am here, and I am solid.

Just like Escaeus.

I fling my dagger toward the closest target as I exhale, praying to the sun above that I might just hit the board this time.

I feel Will and I hold our breath as it flies through the air.

And hits the bullseye with a *clunk*.

I whip my head to meet his eyes, excitement running through my adrenaline filled body.

"I did it!" I scream, jumping into his arms, hugging him so ferociously that there is not an inch between us. "Thank you, thank you, thank you!"

He holds me tight, refusing to let go as he swings me through the air, my feet completely off the ground. "I knew you would. You are the most capable person I know."

He sets me gently back on the snow but does not relent in his grasp. He holds my face between his two hands. "Thank you for allowing me the chance to teach you and witness this."

"There is no one else I'd rather share this moment with." I breathe, our excitement intertwined. Our noses are touching, our breath mingling in the cold air.

"I'd like to kiss you, Penelope," he says quietly, his eyes searching back and forth between mine.

I am taken aback, not having expected this. We've gone so quickly from stolen glances to outright flirting that I feel a bit of whiplash at his confession. Though, I do have one of my own to make, it appears.

"I'd like to kiss you back, Will."

Gently, tentatively, he brings my face closer to his, my lips now hovering just an inch away from meeting his. I can feel my heart beating out of my chest, matching his own quick heartbeat.

I bring my arms around his waist, pulling him in closer as a chill runs through the air between us.

Our lips touch, soft and gentle at first. I melt into his embrace like the warm sea meets the shore.

I nervously bring my gloved hand to run through his shaggy hair.

He pulls away first, our foreheads now touching as we smile together.

"Let's find Haldor and go back home," he whispers gently.

I nod, his lips now finding my forehead to give me another quick kiss.

Home it is.

CHAPTER THIRTY

We hold hands the whole way back.

Haldor leads us this time, Will and I trailing behind as we swing our arms, smiles lighting up our faces.

We can't be bothered to even speak as we make our way to the stronghold, a peace between us that is so evident in the way we walk.

A breeze breaks through the trees, flowing through my curls as I breathe in the crisp mountain air.

I should have known in that moment that this serene environment could only last so long.

As soon as we enter, we hear Kori yelling for William to meet him in the throne room. We share a hesitant look, but he goes on his way, giving my hand a quick squeeze before he lets go. Haldor takes his leave at that, trailing William through the dining hall.

I go downstairs to change, and I'm halfway through my bath before there's a knock on my door. I yell at my surprise guest that it'll just be one minute, and hurriedly wash the rest of my hair and throw on warm, dry clothes.

Selene is standing on the other side of the threshold, an aura of black surrounding her like storm clouds. She smiles at me halfheartedly.

"Can I come in?" Her eyes dart down the hallway, gesturing toward Kori's door as she speaks.

I nod, stating that she may enter, and she smoothly crosses my door and shuts it behind herself.

This is not how I expected her gaining access to my room.

"What is going on?" I ask, confused at her demeanor.

"I can't find Callious," she blurts.

"Did he… leave?" I ask, pausing where I'm at to be still. I knew he wouldn't be staying long, but I never thought he'd leave with things still how they were last night.

"I don't know. I went to bring him breakfast after I ate with you and William, and he was gone."

I sit on my bed, absolutely shocked at the events that have transpired since we've been away.

So much for having another day or two to make things right.

Or give him a piece of my mind.

"Could he be in your… dungeon?" My voice pitches up at the end of that question, unsure if they even *have* a dungeon.

"We have a prison below the mountain, not a dungeon. But no, he's not in there—I checked first. Though, I can only do so much snooping without the reason why being found out around here."

I nod, my heart rate slowing once more. Silence fills

the space between us as my head rushes. "Do you know what Kori wanted from William?"

She shakes her head. "He's only been fuming the last hour or so. His mood is particularly sour, though."

Just like that, there's a soft knock on my door. "Penelope? It's me," Will says quietly through the threshold.

"Come in!" I shout.

He enters, eyeing Selene. "What's this about? A party without me?" He puts his hand over his heart. "I'm wounded, truly."

Selene rolls her eyes at her cousin. "I can't find Callious."

He stops in his tracks, chewing on his bottom lip. "I see. How thoroughly have you looked for him?"

"As much as I'm able," she bites back. "What did Uncle Kori want?"

My eyes dart back and forth, following their exchange. At her question, Will looks at me.

"Actually, I need to talk to Penelope about that. Do you mind giving us a minute, Selene?"

She nods reluctantly, leaving the room. Before shutting the door behind her, she says to me, "I'm sorry he might have left without a goodbye."

A tear threatens to fall down my face, and I glance up at the tall ceiling to keep my emotions hidden inside.

There is a time and a place to cry, and now is not it.

The door clicks shut, and Will comes to sit beside me. Before saying anything, he wipes the tear from my cheek.

"My father knows about Callious." He pauses, letting his words sink in. "He is… not too happy."

I'm stunned, astonishment rising to the surface. "How?"

Will shakes his head, ashamed. "Haldor." He takes my hands, holding them in my lap. "We weren't as inconspicuous as we thought. Unfortunately, even though Haldor particularly likes me, his loyalty is ultimately to my father and Oresteia."

"Where is Callious, then?" I scramble for words, not knowing what to do next.

"He's being held as an ultimatum for you in one of the rooms we keep reserved for guests. My father should be here soon to discuss the details, but before he is, I need to tell you some…"

I interrupt him unintentionally, my thoughts spewing out of me like a rageful sea. "Why does your father hate me so much? Why does it feel as though I've been set up to fail?"

Will is taken aback. "It's not what you've done, but what he believes Paralia has done. Our Kingdoms have been in strife for years. He holds a grudge against your parents for something he thinks they did long ago."

I huff. "What did *we* ever do to *you*?"

He lets go of my hands to wipe them on his lap, now looking me square in the eyes. "My father accused yours of poisoning my mother."

Silence fills the room as I gather the courage to speak.

"Did he?" I whisper, my voice caught in my throat as nerves run throughout my body.

"No," he responds, now taking both of my hands

in his once more. "I spoke the truth when I told you my mother's health degenerated with her mind. The accusation was made from a place of desperation, but my father refuses to let it go."

"His heart was broken—I can see how that would drive him to see things in a warped way. Though, I don't appreciate that grief it has caused all of us for so long." I pause. "So where does that leave us?"

He tucks a strand of hair behind my ear. "I believe when it is my turn to take the crown, I will be able to live side by side with the Frey—peacefully."

I look at him—really look at him—as realization dawns on me and memories flood my mind from what feels like a lifetime ago. "I was the little girl in your story. You were in Paralia. That accusation is the meeting that went wrong."

He blushes, caught. "That might be true."

"Why didn't you tell me?" I ask.

Will sighs. "I didn't want you to feel as though you had to be my friend by force. I wanted this connection to happen naturally, with no prior knowledge keeping us intertwined. It wasn't until a few months ago that I had placed that it was you I had met. Father had begun speaking about Paralia, about the Frey. He told me about his request in bringing one of you here, and that he was choosing the youngest."

He pauses. "Who, he mentioned, was my age. I put the pieces together."

"When I fell into you at the Janus Tree, I thought your eyes looked familiar. But I thought that was just because they look just like your father's."

I ponder, my face turned into a frown, looking off

out my window at the trees swaying, the snow forming circles in the wind. "When I met you that day, it felt like a dream—like déjà vu. To me, it seemed as if our souls had known each other all this time. But, on the other hand, I hardly recall that day as a child at all."

"For me, that day meant everything. I finally had someone to play with—someone to run around with. For you, I'm sure, I was just another kid around your family's palace."

He waits before continuing, "It probably doesn't help that I got verbally corrected that day either, and those moments tend to leave a mark." Will laughs at his own little joke, but I don't find it funny at all.

Not straying from the topic at hand, I get right to the point. "Why did Kori bring me here? What does he truly want from me?"

"He wanted you out of the way—an excuse to have something to hold over your father. I apologize for the way we've made you collateral." He tilts his head, a grin blooming on his face. "Though, I don't apologize that you're here with me now. I've waited years to be reunited with you, dreaming of who you'd be and what you'd be like."

I sigh. "Somehow, Will, you've had me from the very beginning. Even when I was too reluctant to admit it to myself."

We smile at each other softly, and I begin to wonder if he might kiss me again.

I wouldn't mind if he did.

We hold each other's gaze, reality sinking in for the both of us.

"Penelope, I need to tell you something." He lets out a sigh so deep I feel it in my own soul.

My eyebrows furrow. "You can tell me anything."

"I…"

We jump, his words interrupted by the sound of someone banging on my door.

Our heads whip toward the sound, confusion lining our faces.

"William, Penelope," Kori barks. "Get out here, *now.*"

I look at Will, and he looks at me—a silent conversation playing out between us.

I might never know what he was about to let slip from his lips.

Shaking my head slightly to rid myself of those thoughts, I nod and begin steeling my nerves to leave my safe space. I cannot help but drown in the feeling that I may never get to come back.

And ultimately, I ready myself to face Kori—hopefully once and for all.

CHAPTER THIRTY-ONE

My heart races as I leave my room, Will following close behind me. My chest feels as though it might erupt with nerves. Both of my hands are shaking so much that I clasp them together in front of my torso so Kori might not be able to use that fact against me.

I look at him from head to toe, surveying his aura at once so I might grasp his mood completely. Visibly, he's fuming. Color blooms on his pale skin, a vein is popping out of his forehead. His eyes are dilated so much that the ice-blue shade of his eyes is almost nonexistent, giving way to the black of his pupils.

More than that, though, there's an atmosphere surrounding him that makes me feel sick to my stomach. Shades of red extend from his body, mixing and blending into a swirl of energy that makes me nauseous.

Whereas the few auras I've seen previously have been lighter, weaker, Kori's blooms into color so real it's transforming the hallway. The doors no longer look silver, but tinted pink. The walls are no longer white, but blood red.

The window at the end of the hallway looks ominous, a burgundy shaded cloud hovering by the glass panes.

His anger is suffocating, making it hard to catch my breath. Will lays a hand on my lower back, steadying me.

I remind myself to take a deep breath as I stare down the King of Oresteia—in through my nose, out through my mouth.

My pounding heart slows, my hands lessen their shake. I take in Kori's demeanor and remind myself that the only things I can control are my own emotions and how I react to his.

Others can only have as much power over me as I allow them to.

And Kori does not deserve my energy.

"What could you possibly require us both for this urgently?" Will states, staying close to me.

"I hardly require you at all, if not just to prove to you what I've been trying to drill into your skull all along," Kori remarks. His words drip cold venom, his face sour.

I lean into his furious persona, allowing his maroon exterior to bleed into my soul and recharge my own displeasure.

How dare this King pull me away from home on a whim based on an accusation that holds no weight?

I have done all I can to be who he wants me to be here, and yet that is not enough.

And I am so very tired of my worth being determined by another person's dim opinion.

I am finished being seen as someone with nothing to offer.

A quick glance down the hall tells me Selene is nowhere to be found, unless she is tucked away in her room.

Probably a smart decision on her part.

She would kill to wear the shades of red that Kori is exuding.

I snap back to reality—back to the heartless King in front of me and the compassionate prince beside me.

"Give it to me," Kori declares, holding out one pale, calloused hand.

"What?" I ask, taken aback.

"We searched your friend to no avail, which means you have not handed it off to him and it's still in your possession. Give. It. To. Me."

I raise an eyebrow, crossing my arms over my chest. "You're going to have to be more specific."

"The Queen's Heart, you sun-scorched girl! Hand it over or there will be consequences."

I feel Will stiffen beside me. I peek at him, watch him trying to form words. Before he can cut in and make this worse, I respond to Kori's accusation.

I scoff, attempting to appear unamused and indifferent. "I don't have it. I never have."

"Then go ahead and explain why we found your Paralian friend sneaking around the stronghold, looking for a way out? Tell us why he had a letter on his person *from you* discussing the implications of the lost jewel?"

Lost for words, I stutter.

I try to recover, saying, "I did not know Callious would be coming here. Trust me, that was unexpected on my end as well."

Kori steps closer to me, and Will does in tandem, partially shielding me from his father's wrath.

They exchange cold looks, their twin eyes bouncing daggered ice from one to the other. Will matches Kori height to height, glance for glance.

Finally, the King of Oresteia turns his attention back to me. I shudder under his glare.

"I *don't* trust you, and I never will. You have taken advantage of my Kingdom. My workers, my strong-hold, my food, my *son*," he exclaims. "I will not be taken advantage of as well. If you cannot do what has been asked of you, which is to turn over what you've stolen, both you and *Callious* will pay for it."

Kori straightens, now looming over me once more. He sneers, "Your *Kingdom* will pay for it."

He begins to walk away, back toward the foyer. I stand in silence, in shock.

As he reaches the door, he turns to face me once more, resolution all over his face, as if he thought twice about leaving me as he was.

"You have one evening. If you are telling the truth, that you do not have the Queen's Heart in your posses-sion, it would be in your best interest to find it tonight. Both you and Callious will be escorted tomorrow morning at first light back to Paralia. The very moment you enter your Kingdom's gate, war will be issued. You will not have a day to warn your family, to spare your friends."

He looks down his nose at me. "If I were you, I would find it in you to hand over what is rightfully ours before you go. If you refuse to do so, you will want to say your goodbyes. I am being generous in offering you refuge for one more night—do not take this offer lightly."

Kori addresses Will next, leaving me to ruminate on those words. "I expect more from you, William. As a prince, as a son. Do not disappoint me again."

Will's face hardens as his father turns to leave. Before he can exit the door, I exclaim, "What of my friend? Where is Callious?"

Kori's aura broadens into a hot flame tinged with a triumphant gold as his stoic features shape themselves into a wicked grin—one that will replay in my nightmares for the rest of my life.

"You will see him tomorrow."

And with that, he slams the hallway door, leaving Will and I in his wake.

And panic creeping into my mind.

CHAPTER THIRTY-TWO

I face Will, rage building inside of me until I have to resist the urge to scream. The hallway is too empty, my mind too busy. Thoughts race and bounce within, gifting me a pounding headache.

"Your King is… infuriating," I grumble, unable to come up with a better term to fit Kori.

Will paces the length of the hallway before responding, coming back to lay a reassuring hand on my arm. "Callious will be okay until tomorrow. My father won't do anything to him—not without me around, anyway."

"You mean… he might have you give him… an illusion?"

He nods. "I wouldn't put it past him, with how desperate he surely is."

I shake out of his grasp, leaning against the wall behind me. "If that's the case, we need to make sure you aren't around. I need space to think—a place where I can try to figure out what I'm missing. I only have tonight. Otherwise, our Kingdoms are doomed to be enemies forever."

And I will do everything I can to prevent that from happening.

Will hesitates, seemingly more nervous than I've ever seen him. "We could spend the night at the Eremos cottage?"

I shake my head. "I need somewhere new. Ideally somewhere with fresh air—this small space is suffocating me."

Will looks me over. "I have an idea, but you'll need to trust me," he pauses. "You'll also need warmer clothes, as evening is almost upon us."

I glance down at the clothes I threw on when Selene interrupted my bath.

That already feels like a lifetime ago.

"If you'll give me a few minutes to add some layers, I will happily follow you anywhere—even if it's to the ends of Oresteia." I smile at him, hoping he will return the gesture.

Instead, he smirks. "It'll certainly feel like that."

▲▲▲

Back in my room, I already feel more at peace than I did just before. The tall ceilings and vast window allow my breaths to come a bit easier, more relaxed.

I refrain from taking my time picking warmer clothes to wear for whatever Will might have in mind.

I quickly lace up my boots over heavy socks, which are tucked into tight, fleece-lined pants. I'm wearing a thick sweater underneath the coat Will gave me, and the warmth feels both smothering and comfortable at the same time.

I use my fingers to comb through my wild curls, deciding to let them breathe tonight. I flip my hair over my shoulder, put on my gloves last, and make my way back out into the hallway where Will is waiting for me.

Upon first glance, it appears he took the time to change too.

"Do I need anything else?" I ask.

"You're exactly as you need to be," he responds.

"Am I allowed to ask where we are going?"

He grins, linking his arm with mine and steers me toward the hall door.

"I have two spots in mind, but they'll each be a bit of a walk—if that's alright with you."

"I suppose I can be okay with that." I use my shoulder to bump his, making us sway as we walk together.

His presence is so calming.

We go out to the foyer and make our way to the second-floor door that leads outside. It's not yet night, but the afternoon has certainly come and gone. The clouds from earlier have all but dissipated, leaving a clearer, moody sky to be gazed upon.

I breathe in deeply, allowing the crisp, cold air to fill my lungs. My brief headache has subsided, leaving me grateful for the quiet this mountain brings.

I begin to walk in the direction of the garden, as that's the only location I'm aware of outside, but Will makes a quick turn toward the peak, quickly gaining altitude and feet as he scales the cliff's side.

"We're going… up?" I ask, wanting to stop in my tracks.

He looks back at me, gesturing with a hand that I should take it and follow him. I grab hold of his hand with mine, holding on for dear life as we trudge through mounds of snowbanks and rocky surfaces.

"We're going to the top, Penelope. Hold onto me as we go; I won't let you fall."

▲▲▲

Will leads the way, his agile movement like second nature on the terrain. I follow closely behind, my muscles straining against the climb.

"Why is it that I have magic?" I ask, nearly out of breath as we walk.

He ponders this question for a while, maneuvering against the cliffs and jagged rocks. "Perhaps Oresteia knew you would need it."

"I don't understand why," I respond, feeling defeated.

Will squeezes my hand. "I believe you will soon."

We press on together, fueled by the promise of reaching the summit.

After a few hours of relentless climbing, on shaky legs and with airless lungs, we make it to the top.

I make it to the top.

The peak of Escaeus.

The air is thinner up here, requiring me to take deeper breaths and try to slow my heart rate down.

The cloud cover has all but disappeared, leaving a vast view of mountain range after mountain range.

My heart leaps into my throat as Will leads me to the edge of the summit. Never relenting holding my hand, his gentle care in helping me does not go unnoticed.

"Do you want some time alone?" He asks carefully.

"I don't really like heights," I confess, my voice hardly a whisper. "But I would like to be able to say I conquered this."

"Fear is irrelevant." He turns to face me fully, taking my eyes away from the cliff just steps away. "When we are but dust on the wind, no one will spread stories regarding your deepest terrors. Instead, they will speak of your bravery, your kindness, your honesty. They will talk of how you rose above an impossible situation and stayed true to yourself."

I smile at him, my eyes welling at his words. "And you, Will? What will you say of me when I am once again sand on the shore?"

The corner of his mouth lifts, his blue eyes never leaving my own. "I will tell them of the best kiss I've ever received. I will shout from the mountaintops of your perseverance, your sarcasm, your intentionality. I will tell everyone of how radiant you look in every color, but especially in white. And I will never let this Kingdom forget the work you've put in while you've been here—even if it may have been all for naught."

I squeeze his hand, taking a step closer to him so that our foreheads lean together to touch. "And I will tell them of the prince who was *made* to be King. I can only pray to the sun that I live to see the day Oresteia is yours."

Stepping back, I drop our hands. "If I go alone, do you promise to not be too far off? I would hate to fall to my death, and you be unaware."

I laugh, attempting to cover my nerves with that statement. Will, on the other hand, looks at me intently, seriousness never leaving his gaze.

"Penelope, if you fall, I will be right behind you the whole way down."

I look to the horizon, to the steep point of Escaeus. Taking a deep breath, I take one step forward.

And another.

And another.

And another.

One foot after the other, I push myself to get closer and closer. The layer of snow on the peak is lighter here, not quite catching my feet as I walk.

My breath shakes, and I struggle to find sure footing on the edge. Refusing to look down, I survey my surroundings. Though there is no sun, a glimpse of light seems to shine from the atmosphere as I stand.

Visibility stretches for miles and miles, mountain peak after mountain peak growing before my eyes. My hands are tucked warmly in my coat pockets, and I tilt my head upward, allowing the thin air to soak into my very bones.

My curls dance in the wind, flowing freely in front of my face. Though it's harder to breathe, the air feels cleaner up here, and I take in deep breaths like a drowning man in need of oxygen.

Oresteia feels untouched—unblemished.

White powder stretches on for miles and miles, light snow blowing in the breeze in circles and whisps.

Tentatively, I close my eyes. At my back, I know Will is behind me, watching closely. I carefully remove my hands from my pockets, taking my time lest I lose my balance and fall.

Slowly, I lift my arms at my side, allowing them to spread apart from my chest and stretch wide toward the horizon. I tilt my head further back, a smile lining my lips. Finally, I open my eyes, a tear gathering in the corner.

I have swum with creatures unknown, wrestled with waves bigger than man, raced in shifting sand, hiked to a magical tree, faced off with an inhuman King, grappled with things I do not understand.

And yet, here, on this mountain's sacred summit, I am the freest I've ever been.

I am in tune with who I am and who I want to be.

As if Will can hear my train of thought, a pale orange glow begins to seep from behind me, lighting the edges of my hair and the area surrounding me.

His pride for me swells within my heart, warming me from the inside out, rejuvenating me.

Giving me rest.

I turn to look at him, the color of his atmosphere blinding. I smile at him softly, the light surely reflecting off my bronzed face and brown eyes.

"You are the sun personified," he breathes, hardly elevating his voice above a whisper.

My breath hitches.

You are my starlight.

CHAPTER THIRTY-THREE

WE SIT AT THE PEAK OF ESCAEUS FOR A WHILE, TAKING time to breathe in the crisp air, my head on Will's shoulder. He gently rubs his thumb over my hand, our fingers intertwined. Coming from his lips is a melody so soft, the wind threatens to steal his voice before I can hear his hum.

I recognize the tune almost immediately.

"Is that the song you were playing that first day I found you behind the piano?"

He leans into me, wrapping an arm around my cold figure to pull me in closer. "Yes. I wrote it shortly after my father and I's trip to Paralia. It's about a girl with sun kissed skin and golden eyes—a girl whose presence made me feel unrestrained."

Color blooms on my cheeks, my smile unable to be held back. "I wonder who that could be," I remark sarcastically.

He gives my hand a squeeze, lifting it to gently

brush his lips across my knuckles. "If you find her, let me know. I've been aching to get to know her better."

Silence overtakes the space between us, but my mind chooses to not quiet.

A moment to breathe, a moment to escape reality—that's what I need. But now, reality is quickly catching up with me, the weight of the decisions that are meant to be made tonight hitting me.

I have no knowledge of where Callious is other than an empty room. I do not know if he is safe, if he is warm, if he is fed.

I don't know where to start with my accusations about who took the Queen's Heart.

I'm not sure I can handle going back to Paralia with so much still at stake.

I don't want my time here to be cut short.

I don't desire to fight against Will in this war.

Mentally, I kick myself, hating that I am the one who has brought myself to this point. I am the reason this is happening.

If I had never written Callious…

If I had just paid more attention to the signs and conversations at hand…

If I had more to offer this Kingdom and it's King than just small words and surface-level knowledge…

"What are you most afraid of?" Will's murmured voice cuts into my thoughts, distracting me from my hysteria.

He reaches up to tuck a curl behind my ear, his hand lingering on my cheek as I think.

I ponder his question, having never asked myself it before. Finally, an answer comes to me.

"I suppose one could say living in my family's shadow for the rest of my life. I want to feel as if I am still my own person with unique attributes that are worthy of being noticed and needed."

He nods slowly, eyes looking out into the horizon. "I cannot speak for your family, but if I were them, I would recognize just how much you have to offer. Your mind is sharp, your wit is brilliant, and your perseverance is unmatched. I hope, if they do not already, that soon they will be able to see those things in you just as much as I do."

He turns to me, those ice-blue eyes sparkling. "And if you ever felt as though Paralia's heat was no longer what you desired, you are always welcome here."

"Here, as in Oresteia? Or here, as in 'the top of this mountain'? I'm not sure I could last too much longer up here," I joke.

He tilts his head back, laughter now the song coming from his lips. "Here, as in, next to me. You will always have a place by my side."

My lips find his cheek—a light touch connecting us for a moment.

Will stands slowly, making sure his feet are on solid ground. He extends a hand to me, and I take it, rising to my feet.

"Is it time for spot number two?" I ask, curiosity getting the better of me.

He grins at me, a sheepish look spreading across his lips. "Are you okay with a bit more walking?"

"Do I have a choice?" His smile widens. "No."

I scoff, my eyes rolling of their own volition. "Lead the way."

I follow Will back down the mountain slowly but surely, holding his hand and arm through the deep drafts of snow and occasional heavy winds.

As we find our footing back on solid, flat ground in front of the stronghold, evening is now enveloping us in its cool darkness.

Will takes me to the stable, outfitting Agrius quickly with a saddle and bridle. Without further questioning, and with a little bit of help, I hop on his horse first, him following soon behind me.

We trot as we exit the stable and stronghold, and I turn my head to ask Will, "Where are you taking me?"

"I thought it might be about time that you experience our city, especially on a clear night like tonight. In just a few minutes, we will be in Copolis for the evening."

I clap my hands together in delight, nearly falling off in the process. Will quickly corrects my posture, holding me onto Agrius with one hand around my waist, the other hand still on the reins.

After a bit of riding, we find ourselves at Copolis' entrance. A tall, black iron gate separates us from the rest of the city. The metal is lined with warm, yellow lanterns. Though there are two guards stationed to be hidden in the shadows, the ambience is still cozy and inviting.

We swing off Agrius' back, and Will makes quick work of tying him to a post nearby the gate. Patting him on the nose, we are on our way.

The streets are made of cobblestone, and my shoes clack on the uneven rock as we walk past shop after shop.

White banners line the roofs, the triangle shaped fabric waving in the slight evening wind. Snow lays atop the roofs, ice often drifting down in icicles from the corners.

Will says hello to everyone we pass, sounds of laughter and joy flitting through the air to our ears as we walk. Unhurried, we talk to many vendors about what they are selling.

We pass booths lined with spices, scenting the air with warm, robust flavors like cinnamon and ginger.

Another booth holds baby goats, lambs, and sheep. They bleat as we walk past, and the kind owner lets me slip a hand through the fencing to pet their soft noses.

We get caught by an art vendor, selling a variety of painted rocks, logs, and leaves. Her art style is unique, in that she uses naturally found items to create stamps on various sizes of parchment paper. Her colors are richly blended, warm oranges, reds, and yellows mostly at large.

The booth next to hers is covered by precious stones handcrafted into jewelry. A dainty silver ring catches my eye, and I stop to stare. Will continues on his way, not having noticed I paused.

The jewel in the middle is a deep blue, woven by tiny, silvered vines to hold it in place.

The woman standing behind the table notices my attention. "That stone is one of a kind. I've never seen anything like it here."

"It's beautiful. Have you been making jewelry long?"

She shakes her head. "For profit, I only just started. My son decided to enlist in the army. I now require a way to make a living wage with him gone."

I nod, reaching out to touch the ring. "May I?"

She waves her hand at me, giving me permission to slip it on my finger.

A perfect fit, I admire up close the handiwork that must have gone into crafting such a delicate piece.

I take it off and hand it back to her, reluctant to let it go.

"Thank you for your time. I'm Penelope, by the way."

"You can call me K. It was nice to meet you."

I turn my head, seeing Will just a few steps from us, heading back in my direction. His eyebrow is cocked, a questioning look on his face.

The street is bustling with people now, words hardly being heard over the sound of conversations and shouting.

"Did you find something you liked?" He leans in to ask. I see him eyeing K's stand, looking at the table full of precious metals.

"Nothing of note. The vendor was nice."

He smiles, looping his arm through mine. "They all are. You'll find that most sellers are exceptionally proud of what they do and make. Follow me—I want to take you to my favorite vendor."

We weave our way through the busy walkway, our elbows brushing past people of all sorts. Finally, we arrive in front of a small stand covered in a variety of pastries and desserts.

"Penelope, this is Rhea, Tarsha's daughter."

A woman around a decade older than us stands next to her vendor, her light-colored hair bound behind her in a bun. My face lights up, excitement burning in my chest. "Hi Rhea, it's so nice to meet you."

"William, I was wondering when you'd bring this girl to the market." She addresses me now, looking me over. "I've heard so much about you from my mother already. I was getting jealous that she had gotten to meet you and I hadn't!" Rhea exclaims.

She leans in to give me a quick hug, her arms tight around me.

"Rhea owns a bakery here on the square—Rhea's Place. It's Selene and my favorite spot to stop by when we are in the city."

Rhea blushes, obviously swooned by the compliment. "Let me get you two something to drink. Do you want your usual, William?"

"Yes, please. Two cups will do."

I watch as Rhea fills two paper cups with a hot, rich liquid from a stainless-steel container.

The cups steam as she hands them to us, warming us both by their hot temperature. We nod our goodbyes and begin to walk down the street again, trying to find a place to sit.

I breathe in my drink's aroma, a chocolatey undertone filling my body. Will takes a small sip, eyes rolling to the back of his head in delight. I mimic the motion, trying mine for the first time.

The drink is just as rich as it is dark, coating my tongue and throat in its warmth and intensity.

"She calls this hot chocolate. It's especially good on a cold, winter night."

I look down at my cup, swirling the heavy liquid around before taking another sip. "It's heavenly."

Suddenly, the street goes pitch black. All the lanterns are snuffed out, the shop lights have gone off. I look at Will in shock, but he's just smiling at me as if this was expected.

A soft melody drifts through the air, songs on strings now playing loudly within the market. Someone begins singing along, words indecipherable in comparison to the volume of the instruments.

Will takes my cup from my hands, setting them both down on the ground. He stands, holding out a hand to myself. I take it, rising with him.

"While we are here," he whispers to me, "we should dance."

The darkness envelopes our bodies as the soft melody bounces off the walls of the shops next to us. There is a peace in the air—a tranquility I have not yet known.

Will draws me in close, his hands on my waist. I find my arms wrapping around his neck, drawing me even closer. The darkness paints an illusion that it is just us on this night-kissed street.

We stand facing each other, our gazes locked in a silent understanding as we begin to sway with the rhythm of the music. One of his hands finds mine, our palms interlocking in an intimate embrace as we wholly surrender to the violinist's song.

Our steps are unhurried, each movement slowing down time as we breathe in this space together.

"I was never taught to dance," I proclaim, embarrassed once again by the lack of training in my upbringing compared to his.

"Then let me lead," he says, his nose a hair's width away from my own.

Slowly, he spins me around. With care, he dips me. Between us, there is a communication that only we know. We speak through the touch of our fingers, the brush of our bodies, the light in our eyes.

Our proximity is palpable, the air between us filled with an electric tension that crackles and hums its own song.

Thoughts flit through my mind, reminding me of the task at hand and what's at stake. Yet, at this moment, I am content to simply be. My heart begs me to lose myself in this shared space.

As the music swells and fades, we remain intertwined in our own private world, moving together in perfect harmony. In this fleeting moment, time seems to stand still, granting me a glimpse of what living truly is.

"Look up," Will breathes.

I do, my eyes now locked onto the sky.

The star-flecked sky.

I gasp, the beauty of what I'm seeing catching me off guard.

"It's beautiful," I murmur. I look at Will, only to find that his eyes are on me.

"I know."

Blushing fiercely, I lean my head on his shoulder.

Time is frozen solid as we hold each other beneath
a velvet-colored blanket of night, the two of us viewing
a tapestry woven of pure starlight and constellations.

CHAPTER THIRTY-FOUR

Eventually, we make our way back to the stronghold, silently slipping through the front door and through the foyer to the royal hall.

Will walks me to my door, taking a moment to lean against my door frame and caress my cheek.

"I enjoyed my evening with you," he confesses, his eyes locked onto mine.

"I do hope it wasn't our last evening together," I remark, worry catching up to me.

He leans forward to brush his lips against my forehead, soothing my anxiety. "Get some rest. I'll see you in the morning."

With that, he turns and sneaks into his own bedroom, leaving me to mine.

My room is cloaked in darkness, save for the faint glow filtering from the stars outside my window. The evening is still just as clear as it was when we left the city, the stars seemingly smiling at me as if we share a secret.

I quickly get ready for bed, the hot bath I take a slight reprieve from the chill that was present outside.

As I lie down to sleep, my senses are overrun with thoughts and ideas.

How am I supposed to rest tonight, knowing this is my last and final chance?

I've failed.

After tossing and turning restlessly, I make my way across my room to grab my leather-bound journal from my desk drawer.

I clutch it tightly to my chest, brow furrowed in distress and exhaustion as I make my way back to my bed.

Sitting on top of the rumbled covers, I wrap my blanket around my shoulders. My pen hovers over a fresh, blank page of my journal, words refusing to materialize despite desperation clawing at my brain.

I sigh in frustration, squeezing my eyes shut in a desperate attempt to concentrate on the racing thoughts stuck inside my brain.

"Come on, Penelope. Just write!" I whisper to myself, fingers clutching tightly around my pen.

With a shaky hand, I begin to scrawl on the page, my handwriting the most uneven and jagged it's ever been.

There is no meticulous form of words here, no careful consideration of whether what I'm writing makes sense.

I write about my time here—about Oresteia. I write about William, about Selene. I write my fears and my uncertainties, feeling as though the weight of two Kingdoms is pressing upon my shoulders.

I take a ragged breath.

I write about Kori, about his cold-like exterior and the words he's spoken to me and about me. As I write, I think back to our most recent interaction and the aura he presented.

Tinged with gold, I mull over to what that could mean from someone like him, when his usual aura is icy and carefree.

When I think of the color gold, I think of winning.

Victory? Success? Triumph?

I ponder, thinking of the Queen's Heart – surely stolen by someone of royal blood.

Why else would Oresteia grant me this gift to see emotions so vividly?

Kori has the most to gain from war—being that he is finally able to fight for this grudge he's been holding onto for twelve years.

What if he took it?

What if it's never been lost?

Why else would the King of Oresteia be adorned in a golden atmosphere, topped with a smirk and pride evident in his voice?

It hits me with resolution—no doubt in my mind.

Kori stole the Queen's Heart.

That's why he's asked William to keep me busy.

It must also be why he's never tried talking to me about what I know and has been reluctant to work with me or see me.

It makes so much sense now as to why there's no record of someone making a fake, or of stealing the real thing.

I can't believe I didn't see it sooner.

A newfound fire burns in my heart, ready to stand against him tomorrow. I toss my journal aside, burrowing into my covers with resolution.

Darkness finally consumes me, lulling me into a place of fitful rest.

I find myself standing on the edge of Escaeus, a violent wind whipping around me, threatening to knock me off my feet.

There's a sound behind me and I turn, too quickly for the small platform I'm standing on. Kori is at my back, his eyes glowing a menacing blue.

"I know it was you," I say, but my voice drowns out in the wind.

He takes a step closer, cocking his head to the right. His eyes bore into my soul, chilling me from the inside out.

"Do you?" He remarks, just before overpowering me and pushing me closer to the edge of the mountain.

He leans in, a whisper on his lips. "You. Know. Nothing."

I grapple at the air as I'm pushed off the cliff, arms flailing at my side.

A blood-curdling scream tears through the silence of the night, jolting me awake. Sweat forms on my brow, my body twisted in the sheets I'm lying in. My heart is racing in my chest, whimpers caught in my throat.

It was just a nightmare…

Just a nightmare…

My breathing is ragged as I struggle to shake off the lingering fear stuck in my mind.

My door cracks open slightly, light from the hall

filtering in. Will pops into my room abruptly, his hands lifted in defense, as if ready to fight at a moment's notice.

Seeing the state I'm in, concern etches on his face as he runs to my side, hurriedly wrapping his arms around my trembling form.

"You're brave," he reminds me. "You're alive."

I bury my face into the crook of his shoulder, breathing in his warm, vanilla scent. His comforting embrace calms my beating heart, air once again filling my lungs.

I struggle to find the words to describe the short scene that plagued my dreams, my voice hardly a whisper.

Will strokes my hair gently, the strands matted to my forehead. His touch is a soothing relief to my frazzled nerves.

I cling to him in the silence, my fingers curling into the fabric of his shirt desperately, fear encompassing me as if he might let go.

"Will you stay?" I murmur.

He blinks in the darkness, as if taken aback that I would have to ask. "Of course."

Will reaches for my journal lying forgotten on the bed, his fingers tracing the smooth design on the cover.

"Did you try writing about it?"

I swallow. "I think writing about it all is what caused the nightmare. It was on my mind just before I drifted off."

My eyes meet his, a glimmer of gratitude shining in my gaze.

Determination flickers across my features, remembering the conclusion I came to just a bit before my terror. I rise from the bed, untangling myself from his embrace. I cross the room to my desk again, retrieving my dagger from its drawer.

Just because I'm ready to face Kori tomorrow does not mean my accusation will change the course of events unfolding before me.

"Spar with me," I say, moving to the middle of the room. "If we are to go to war, I want to be ready."

Will stands, taking his place across from me. "You're lucky I never leave my room without my dagger."

He unsheathes it, righting his posture and holding it up in a ready stance.

With a swift motion, I fix my gaze on his hand, steadying myself.

In the stillness of night, the sound of metal slicing through the air fills the room as we par and block each other's blows.

Each hit is a release of pent-up fear, defiance against his father's name, a stand in readiness for what's to come.

Will matches my fight blow for blow, admiration caught in his eyes.

We pause, chests gasping for air.

"Thank you… for being here."

He puts his dagger away, crossing the room in a few swift strides. He grabs my arms with care, gently holding me steady.

With a light touch, he presses a kiss to my forehead.

"Whatever tomorrow may bring."

CHAPTER THIRTY-FIVE

I STIR FROM MY FITFUL SLEEP, FINDING MYSELF TANGLED in a web of blankets. I blink away the remnants of my restless dreams, my heart still racing with echoes of the night's terrors.

With a sigh, I push myself upright, rubbing the sleep from my eyes as I survey my surroundings. Will is nowhere to be found, the floor beside me lying empty. The room is shrouded in silence, making me uneasy.

As I reach to straighten my sheets, my hand brushes against something small and folded. I lift the corner of my blanket, my eyes widening in surprise as I discover a note lying on my bed.

My heart quickens with anticipation as I unfold it, my eyes scanning the hastily scribbled writing.

Penelope,

I'm sorry to be off before you wake, but there's a conversation I must have.

I will see you before you go.
—William

My heart swells as I struggle to come to terms with the waking world around me.

As I get ready, I realize I need to pack all my belongings before facing off with Kori, lest I be forced to leave without them.

Not that I have much to take back with me in the first place.

Hurriedly, I throw my few items back in the bag I traveled here with. I'm wearing cold-weather pieces from my closet here for the journey, but I expect I'll need to shed a few layers once we reach Paralia.

Suns above, I'm going back to Paralia today.

My time here has been cut short, seemingly by the person who is to blame for it all in the first place.

The room is dimly lit, the air hanging heavy with grief as I mourn what could have been in the rest of my time here. My movements are sharp and deliberate as I zip up my bag and survey the space.

A storm rages within me, bitter winds violently whipping around inside my heart and head as I prepare for what I need to say to Kori.

And how he might react to it.

As I look around, memories flood my mind. Departing this place leaves me feeling hollow, helpless.

I pause as I lay eyes on the dried flowers Will gave me early on into my time here, the stalks still sitting in their vase.

My eyes burn with unshed tears, knowing I cannot take those with me, or else they will be broken beyond repair by the time we reach Paralia's shores.

I shoulder my bag, sealing away the promise of another tomorrow here. This life was just beginning to feel like my own.

With one last glance around the room, I steel my nerves.

The mountains do not apologize for taking up space, and neither will I.

▲▲▲

I begin to walk to the throne room with my bag around my shoulder, unsure of where I might find Kori lurking.

Before I can leave the hallway, I hear a shout come from Will's room. He bursts out of the door aggressively, practically falling into my arms as I leap back and yelp in surprise.

"Will!" I exclaim, catching him before he falls.

I've never seen him so unsteady.

"Penelope," he rights himself, brushing off his pants and straightening his shirt.

"I apologize for my abrupt demeanor. I wasn't expecting to see you like this—I thought I had a bit more time to prepare what I wanted to say."

"What do you mean?" I respond.

His eyes fill with tenderness as he reaches into his pants pocket, holding something with his left hand.

I give him a questioning look, my hand still holding onto his arm.

"I believe in you. There is no distance I would not travel for you, to you. Learning to know you has been a gift—one I hope to continue receiving for the rest of my life. I don't know what tomorrow will look like, and I don't know what war will bring. I beg the stars that you will not forget me as we part."

He pauses, holding open his palm in front of me. "Not for a moment have I forgotten you since we met some years ago, and I do not plan on starting now."

I look down at his open hand, revealing a delicate silver ring.

The ring from the market.

I gasp, my eyes searching his as he places it on my first finger, opposite the hand that holds my Frey family ring.

"It's been enchanted so that as long as you are wearing it, you will never be denied entry to the Oresteian walls." Will says this apprehensively, as if this fact might scare me away.

"It's beautiful. How did you…" I start, unable to comprehend the lengths he must have gone through this morning to secure this ring for me.

He softly smiles at me, his head tilting to the right.

"I don't know if I'll see you again before you go," he begins.

I shake my head. "I have words I need to share with your father. It might be best if you aren't present."

He nods, contemplating this. "I *will* see you again."

I bring my hand to his cheek, letting it rest there and say everything I cannot. "Goodbye, Will."

He shakes his head ever so slightly, looking as if he cannot bear to say another word. He slips back into his room, shutting the door quietly behind him.

As I move on toward the throne room, I realize

with heavy longing that I may have just bid him farewell forever.

With war on the horizon, there's no telling whether we will see or speak to each other ever again.

Perhaps we will meet again on the battlefield.

I shudder at the thought.

Kori is standing in the middle of the throne room as I enter, with Haldor and Callious by his side. I share a look with Callious, raising an eyebrow at him to ask if he's okay. He gives me one nod, his hands seemingly tied behind his back.

I shoot my glare back at Kori, trying to look unbothered. He looks down his nose at me.

"I take it you've decided to not yield?"

I stand my ground, attempting to look back at him with an equal amount of distaste.

"It is not me who needs to yield."

Kori cocks an eyebrow at me, his wary face bewildered.

It appears I've caught him off guard.

"I'm innocent," I declare, my voice ringing with authority and power. "But you, King Kori, are not."

Haldor and Callious gasp at my accusation. Kori, though, appears unmoved. His gaze is just as cold and calculating as always.

"Excuse me?" he asks, silence now filling the space.

I hesitate, shifting from foot to foot. I'm not sure what response I was expecting, but it was not that.

My bag begins to lay heavy on my shoulder. "I believe…" I start, my voice caught in my throat.

Stand tall.

Fire once again starts to burn in my veins as I'm

reminded of all the people at risk should war break out between our two Kingdoms.

With renewed sense of purpose, I stare down Kori, coming face to face with him as I move to where he stands. His eyes burn with rage the closer I come.

"I believe *you* took the Queen's Heart, King Kori. No one stands to gain as much as you do in this looming war. You refuse to let go of your grudge against my father. You refuse to admit that you were *wrong.* Your pride will cost our Kingdoms hundreds of lives, if not thousands."

My confidence swells within my chest, begging me to continue unwavering. "You rule with an iron fist—thriving on fear and anger. I will praise the sun for the day William takes over in your stead—the day Oresteia is left in much more capable hands."

His brows furrow into a deep crease, casting a shadow over his fuming gaze.

"You believe *I* stole my own artifact?"

I nod, not backing down from where I stand.

"I haven't been able to access my magic in months. My Kingdom stands to fall just as yours does. I do not care for the opinion of a little girl who hardly has anything to offer. You are here because *I* warranted it, hoping your family would see reason before I am left do what I must. Your time here has taught you nothing."

"If you didn't take it…" I falter, his words and conviction sinking in as my shoulders curve inward, protecting myself from his verbal blow.

I was wrong.

"If you didn't take it, I don't know who did."

"Me, Penelope," a voice cuts in from behind me. "It was me."

I whip my head around to the sound, shock nearly making me fall to my knees.

Selene.

CHAPTER THIRTY-SIX

The air stands still as we look her over, both of us clearly shocked at her admission and entrance.

Kori barks a laugh behind me, short and quick, making me flinch at the sound.

"Selene, don't be dense." He shifts where he stands, a hand going into the pocket of his pants as if shaken.

Her eyes move to meet mine, reluctance hidden in her dark gaze.

"Selene…" I whisper, my voice tinged with disbelief.

She rushes to me, her hands clutching mine in haste.

"I'm so sorry." Her words slur together, as if she cannot speak fast enough. "I never meant for you to find out this way. William came to me, telling me you were leaving this morning, and I didn't want you to be blamed for something I did…"

The air in the throne room chills, ice filling my lungs as I try to breathe.

"Will... knew?" I ask, my chest rising and falling in fast succession as my breathing quickens.

How could I be so stupid?

Footsteps coming from the door catch my attention. Will runs in, looking back and forth between me, Selene, and his father.

Anguish fills his features as he comes to a stop to assess the room. Haldor and Callious look at us from the corner, standing still as if to not draw attention to themselves.

My heart pounds in my chest, feeling both crushed and confused.

I look back and forth between Selene and Will and watch them silently exchange a conversation.

"William," Kori announces. "So kind of you to join us. Please, explain."

Will opens his mouth to respond, but Selene cuts him off with a wave of her hand. She moves past me, focusing solely on Kori now.

"It would be best, Uncle Kori, if I did." She waits for his approval, continuing once she receives a sharp nod from him. Her voice trembles with emotion, but she stands tall. "I want to fight. I thought if war was imminent... that you might... allow me to join the army's ranks. I never meant for it to go on this long, or to drag Penelope into this mess.

"As soon as she got here, I realized my mistake, that I had gone too far. I knew that if you were going to allow me to fight, you would have sent me to the gate by that time. I was hoping to return the Queen's Heart to its rightful place with no one the wiser, so she could be on her way, but her and William were always around, and I never got a chance to swap them back…"

She addresses me, heartfelt emotion lingering in her eyes. "I just wanted to be somewhere I felt like I belonged. I'm deeply sorry you got dragged into my own antics."

The air is thick with tension as the weight of the truth hangs between us all like a storm cloud.

Selene reaches for me, but I recoil, my eyes brimming with tears at the realization of what they've done to me. I shake my head in disbelief, now locking eyes with William.

"What part did you play in all of this? Have you just been leading me along, as if I would not suffer for her decisions?"

He steps forward, his expression pained as his hand moves forward to touch me. His hand retracts soon after though, as if he thinks better of that decision.

His eyes harden just slightly, the glare looking more like Kori's by the minute.

"I didn't know at first." Will runs a hand through his hair, thinking through his next words. "I only came to the realization soon after you got here, Penelope. It didn't make sense for it to be anyone else. I confronted Selene this morning, begging her to come forward so you might not pay the price, hoping this wrong could be righted."

He hesitates, shifting from foot to foot. "I do not regret keeping this secret for her, though." His gaze now addresses Kori behind me. "I believe Selene would be a valuable asset to our force. She was made for this position in this place—you are harming her, and us, by keeping her from it."

William now looks back to me, a rueful expression filling his eyes. "I couldn't tell you. At first it was because I didn't know where your loyalties lie, but later because I didn't know how to tell you. There's so much you don't know about us, about Oresteia… I was scared you would not understand."

I shoot daggers at him, unamused by his ramblings. My voice fills with accusation as I turn to face him fully. "I have *always* been on your side, on your team. I would have never betrayed your trust in me. I *understand* how it feels to not be welcome where you're meant to be. I might even understand better than you do."

I look back and forth between Will and Selene now, their appearances brimmed with remorse. "I trusted you both wholeheartedly, and I see now that was a mistake."

Kori cuts in, preventing me from saying more.

"Where is the Queen's Heart?"

Selene bows her head slightly, shuffling forward warily. Out of her pocket, she pulls out a round diamond about the size of her palm. The white shine is clear, the light from the room reflecting off it.

We all freeze as we look at the jewel resting there, as if its short disappearance did not almost cause the deaths of many.

Kori snatches it out of her hand but takes his time to replace it within the Queen's Crown. As soon as it is in its rightful place, surrounded by the silver vines of the crown, it appears as though Kori breathes again, his head falling back, relieved.

He pinches the skin between his eyes with his fingers.

"Selene," Kori pauses, regaining his composure. "Your disobedience against me and disregard for our Kingdom, is the exact reason why you will *never* be allowed to fight within our ranks. We do not accept those we cannot rely on, and you have proven to be exceptionally unreliable. You do not think before you act, and that is going to get you, and those around you, killed."

"King… Is there anything I can do to change your mind?" Her voice is hardly a whisper, her eyes turned downcast toward the floor.

Kori considers this for only a second, thinking quickly. "The only way you will ever see battle is if William is sent to the lines first." His tone is filled with resolution, his word final. "Tomorrow we will decide your fate."

She nods, a tear falling from her face to the floor. Selene runs out of the room, composure broken as Kori addresses William.

Kori's expression is grave as he regards his son, disappointment evident in his eyes.

"I am deeply disturbed by your actions, William."

They stare each other down. William stands tall, a hint of defiance in his stance.

"I assure you, King; I have acted in the best interest of our Kingdom."

Kori's gaze hardens, his displeasure intensifying at William's words.

"Your *actions*, son," Kori spits, "have brought us nothing but chaos and unrest. It is clear you care nothing for your people, your family, or the duty you hold as heir."

"I strive to uphold my own honor and integrity, father. Keeping Selene's secret is not something I assessed would demote either of those qualities. I have made my decision, and I stand by it."

"The burden of leadership is not one I will have you take lightly. There will be consequences to your actions, lest you believe you are clear of charges. You and I will continue this later, lest it be reported back to Paralia's ruler."

Finally, Kori's eyes meet mine. Haldor steps forward with Callious, realizing they no longer need to stay in the shadows for this exchange.

Before Kori can address me, I speak my truth, my voice amplified so all in this space can hear.

"I will not forget what has transpired here, King Kori." I wait, my stance confident and filled with power. "I'm ready to go."

With that, I turn and walk away, leaving William and Kori standing in that empty throne room, their hearts surely in turmoil and agony. Haldor and Callious follow closely behind me, the sound of our footsteps against the floor echoing through these haunted halls.

CHAPTER THIRTY-SEVEN

THE THREE OF US BEGIN OUR LONG JOURNEY BACK, MY bag around my shoulder and hurt in my heart.

We exchange a long look at each other as we walk down the cobblestone path, out the stronghold entrance, past the guards, and into the rest of Oresteia below, Escaeus looming behind us.

Haldor takes time to unbind Callious' hands. Callious rubs at his wrists, raw marks present on each.

"We will travel to the Oresteian gate today. From there, you two are on your own for the Stenos Isthmus," Haldor says, looming a few steps ahead of Callious and me.

"It appears you've drawn the short end of the stick in order to be the one to deliver us from the stronghold," I respond, hardly keeping up to his long- legged strides.

Haldor turns, barely looking at me over his shoulder as if in assessment. "I volunteered."

"To take us?" I question, disbelief evident in my tone.

He continues on his way. "I've become rather fond of watching you embarrass yourself. And your friend put up a good fight attempting to be released."

Callious, who has been silent for our entire encounter thus far, huffs. He mumbles something under his breath, his head hanging low in defeat.

I scoff. "I'm glad I could provide you with some entertainment."

We walk in a slightly unpeaceful quiet, our shoes scuffling along the mountainous path. The snow is muddy and packed down under our feet, causing us to slip occasionally where the powder becomes ice.

The air is brisk, but the bite of the wind is not a chilly cold as it has been on previous days. Instead, it is a mild rawness that only feels sharp against my nose and ears, which are unfortunately exposed to the infrequent breeze.

I continuously attempt to make some sort of contact with Callious as we walk, whispering his name and shoving my elbow into his. Nevertheless, he persists in keeping a downturned persona, refusing to look at me or speak.

The miles are long, and my feet are tired. I did not realize when I rode into the Kingdom all those days ago on Agrius just how swiftly and fast that horse could move through the rough and uneven landscape. It takes all my attention to stay upright on my feet, let alone move forward at their pace.

At last, our trio of unlikely travelers arrives at the Oresteian gate just before mid-afternoon. My heart pounds in anticipation as Haldor continues to walk to talk to the two guards on duty, each dressed in a richly colored onyx shirt and pants.

Surely they know who he is.

As he addresses them, I look around. A large watch tower looms above us overlooking the isthmus. Its weathered stone walls are a testament to the time that has passed and the trials it has surely seen.

At its base, a sturdy iron door serves as an entrance, guarded by the two men here with us. There's a broad platform at the top, with more guards stationed there. Lamps hang from the railing up above, casting a warm glow against the rough stone walls.

The Kingdom's land stretches out in all directions from here, an endless white void as far as my eyes can see.

There are many dark-clothed men milling about, surely here to prepare for what we thought would be upcoming battle. Tents are stationed in various places, a few standing upright with the flaps wide open.

They don't seem too concerned about war.

"State your business," the man on the right barks, his hand set on the sword hanging at his side.

Haldor steps forward, his voice steady and unwavering. "I am Haldor, Guard of the King." He removes his cloak from around his neck, showcasing to the two men in front of us what looks to be a type of branding on his collarbone.

From where I stand, I can hardly make out the picture depicted. It appears to be black ink on his skin, starkly contrasting against the paleness of his neck.

"Traveling with me are two exiles, having finished

their duties in Oresteia. They require use of the Isthmus immediately."

They look upon his neck, nodding to what they see. I attempt to peer over his shoulder to catch a better look, but he replaces his cloak back to where it belongs before I can.

The two men regard Haldor for a long moment, their gazes penetrating, yet unreadable.

Why must this be so complicated?

The two straighten their posture, standing tall. "Very well. You may enter—but know that your presence here does not guarantee safety. The Isthmus is long and treacherous, and night will soon be on its way."

Haldor gives them a short bow, now addressing us.

"I've taken you as far as I'm able."

With that, he turns on his heel and walks toward the erected tents, surely going to find a place to stay for the night.

I look at Callious, hoping to find an inkling of the fire left within him, but instead, my eyes are met with a wounded dog of a human being.

Frustrated, I shake my head.

I suppose that means I'm on my own.

I square my shoulders, ready to continue on our way. The tall iron fence looms over us as the guards open the barrier. They watch us carefully, their eyes filled with scrutiny as we walk past.

The Stenos Isthmus takes shape ahead of us as our feet meet its uneven soil. The narrow strip of land holds promise for the journey to come, even though my body is already weary from the trek we've already done.

The light, icy Khionean Sea stretches in a vast expanse on either side of the isthmus, reflecting the gray sky above. Soon, the Khionean Sea will meet the Neronian Sea with a kiss—light blue waves intermixing with dark waters.

The rhythmic lapping of waves against the shore provides a soothing melody to our walk, filling me with a renewed sense of determination to finish this journey.

The isthmus is a painting of change, its terrain shaped by constantly modifying waves and the meeting of shoes to soil. Cliffs rise from the shoreline on either side, their weathered demeanor bearing witness to the relentless power of our seas.

The first few miles are riddled with slightly melting snow, the piles more mud than anything else. As we move toward the middle of the isthmus, closer to Paralia, the murky slush turns to soil, and then to sand under our feet.

At the heart of the Stenos Isthmus lies a sense of unity and connection between our two Kingdoms as the land and sea merge as one. The ground serves as a bridge between two distant shores, two distant kings. It's a space where we collide and merge, our worlds connected as one.

As I walk and listen to the sound of the waves on either side of us, I'm reminded of home. I cannot help but feel a sense of awe and reverence for what both Paralia and Oresteia have to offer.

It is not a weakness that we are vastly different.

Instead, it could create a perfect harmony between us, should we choose to lean into the opportunities it presents our Kingdoms.

As we walk, I realize the silence between Callious and me has become a hum I can no longer avoid.

The air is filled with a gentle lapping of the waves, the temperature quickly rising as we make it to the middle of the isthmus.

I begin to shed layers, taking off my cloak and coat from around my torso. I wrap them both around my bag, but the items are beginning to bear too much weight to my shoulder. I swap which arm it hangs on, freeing up my right hand to tap Callious on the shoulder.

He glances up at me, his shoulders slumped, his eyes clouded with sorrow as he struggles to maintain eye contact.

"Tell me what you need," I whisper, my voice hardly rising above the sea.

Callious shakes off my touch, his eyes now on the horizon coming into view in front of us. The sun is slowly beginning to shine from behind clouds above, its rays drifting into our skin.

Though the evening is surely starting to be upon us, and our bones are weary from travel, our steps quicken of their own volition as the Paralian gate glides into view at the end of the narrow straight.

"I failed," he admits, his voice gravelly from disuse.

I cock my eyebrow at him, confused. "Failed?"

He laughs, the sound dry and empty. "You didn't need me. You've never needed me." Callious shakes his head, his dark hair drifting in front of his forehead in messy locks. "I had begun to think of myself as your savior—the only person who truly knew and understood you. But seeing you with them, seeing how much they cared for you…"

His eyes finally meet mine. "I did underestimate you, Nelly. I assumed you wouldn't be able to handle yourself there, that you would need someone available to tell you what to do and where to go. And when I realized my mistake and tried to leave, Kori found me and seized me before I could silently correct my blunder.

"I have put you through a world of hurt, an immense amount of confusion and difficulty. Because of my presence, you were forced to leave a place that I truly believe you considered home, or at the very least, had started to. I don't blame you if you hate me, for all I've done to you."

I clutch his hand, my expression earnest and true. "I could never hate you, Cal. Your presence might have brought upon my leave," I frown, "but it seems as though my time there was coming to an end anyway."

He brings a hand to my chin, lifting it to meet his gaze. "They'll come for you."

I shake my face from his grasp, my eyes set to the sun dipping below the horizon, the Paralian gate not too far ahead. "I'm not sure I want them to."

CHAPTER THIRTY-EIGHT

When Callious and I finally arrive at the Paralian gate, he decides to stay behind to receive a briefing on what he missed while he was away. He seems anxious to return to Komeus, and I don't blame him given the recent events that have transpired.

I continue on, pushing through the fatigue. Deep into the cover of night, the evening breeze cool on my skin, I make it to the palace at last.

I slip into our foyer unnoticed, my weary footsteps echoing off the marble floors as I take in the familiar surroundings. The scent of sea salt fills the air, a comforting reminder of the home I once knew. I pause for just a moment, closing my eyes and letting it wash over me like a warm embrace.

With a renewed sense of determination, I set off down the hall, my steps purposeful as I make my way through the labyrinth of passages. Each turn brings me closer to my destination, my heart racing with anticipation of finally reaching my bedroom.

Finally, my door looms before me, my gateway to a sanctuary. With tired bones and a trembling hand, I reach out and push it open, revealing the colorful haven within. The room is bathed in soft lamplight, as if it's been waiting for me.

I step inside, my eyes drinking in the sight of my bed, covered in plush pillows and light blankets. Without hesitation, I throw my bag to the ground, cross the room, and collapse into the soft mattress. The sheer canopy covering my bed lays softly against the wood frame, enclosing me.

I let out a sigh as I bury my face into the pillows. Tomorrow the weight of the day's trials will drown me, but for tonight, rest is the only thing on my mind. I am home at last, surrounded by the comfort and security of this palace.

▲▲▲

I enter my father's study early the next morning. The room is grand, larger than necessary, adorned with tapestries depicting scenes of Paralia. Father sits at his desk, the morning light casting a glow off the light wood of the piece.

King Zannan is engrossed in the affairs of his kingdom, so much so that he hardly notices when I step into the room.

I stand before him, both frustrated and determined. "Father."

He looks up, surprised. "Pen, what are you doing back on our shores? The timeframe given has hardly come to pass and I did not hear that you were leaving."

"I was sent home. King Kori no longer required my presence."

He shoots up from his chair, overtaking the space.

"What does this mean? Did you find the artifact? Have you done what you were meant to do?"

I glance down at my feet, forgetting I must make this admission. "No, father. There was quite a big misunderstanding, which led to me being discharged. I…" I pause. "I do believe his intentions are still set on war."

My father picks up a stack of papers from his desk, only to throw them down in anger. I flinch, having not prepared myself for this sort of reaction.

He chuckles humorlessly to himself. "I should have known better than to send you. These affairs require knowledge, discretion—something you unfortunately lack."

I balk at him. "Discretion? Is that so? You've kept me in the dark, father, my whole life! You've done nothing but treat me like a child while you allow my siblings to be fully briefed on the knowledge of our world and surroundings!"

He wrings his hands through his dark hair, quickly losing his composure. "I have always known you were not ready for the burdens of this court. There are things at play that you cannot possibly understand."

"If I lack basic understanding, it is because of *you*."

"Do not lecture me on understanding. I have spent my life in this position, preparing for every possible scenario I might be presented with."

My voice rises. "Preparing? You've done nothing but avoid the inevitable. We have been in conflict with Oresteia for *years*. What is this rumor regarding you poisoning the Queen of Oresteia?"

Father sits back down into his chair, shoulders slumped.

"Kori has obviously tainted your reality. I do hope you do not believe that to be true. You may not see it now, but everything that has transpired has been done out of protection for our Kingdom, our people, and our family."

"I don't want your protection, father. I want your trust. I want to prove to you that I am capable. I thought that by going to Oresteia, you might begin to see me as an asset rather than a burden." I shake my head. "I can see now that I was wrong."

He snorts at me. "It's painfully obvious that you are not as capable as you'd hope. I gave you specific instructions upon this assignment—search for what was lost, write immediately. You could not handle these simple terms. How am I meant to believe you could handle the affairs of Paralia?"

"You didn't prepare me! You didn't verse me on the history between our two Kingdoms. You hardly sent me off with a goodbye at all!" I cannot hide my anger, frustration bursting at the seams of my heart.

He attempts to respond, but I cut him off before he can utter a word.

"I don't know why I bothered coming in here at all. You will never see me as a potential heir, or as a daughter with something to offer. You are blind to the person standing before you, and someday, I hope you realize what you've forsaken."

At that, I turn on my heel and rush out of the room.

▲▲▲

Of their own volition, my feet take me swiftly to the shore of the Neronian sea, my cares left behind.

The gentle rhythm of the warm waves provides a soothing soundtrack for my soul. Tears stream softly down my face, the taste of salt in my mouth.

I gaze out at the vast expanse of the Neronian, lost in thought.

I run my fingers through the cool sand, feeling its gritty texture against my skin, letting it ground me.

Amidst the chaos and uncertainty of these last few weeks, there has always been one thing ever present and constant: myself.

The water stretches endlessly into the horizon in front of me, its surface shimmering in the sunlight. Since I've been gone, it remains both changed and the same all at once.

There is something about the sea in that regard that speaks to me, reminding me of my place. Its vastness nudges my mind that there are infinite possibilities that lie ahead, endless opportunities waiting to be lived.

At that moment, I fully understand why Selene took the Queen's Heart. She was being met with no after no for the one thing she really wanted, and she thought it was within her grasp to have it.

Truthfully, I do recognize why she did it. I just wish she had trusted me enough to let me know.

It's possible I would have done the same thing, had I been in her place.

The sand next to me shifts suddenly with the weight of another person sitting beside me.

I hardly glance at him, my brain recognizing the familiar rise and fall of his chest.

"Everett," I say. "Have you come to taunt me?"

"No. Rather, I've come to tell you that it's about time father is put in his place by one of us. You didn't hear it from me, but I do believe old age is working against him."

He nudges me with his elbow, and a smile plays lightly on my lips.

"You were brave for going, Penelope. None of us would have known what to do, lest of all myself."

Silence overtakes us as the waves continue hitting the shore. "What do you know of the rift between our Kingdoms?"

"I know that it has caused both of our parents years of grief. We once had a thriving relationship with Oresteia, one I always hoped to reinitiate when I received the crown."

I nod, my eyes still on the horizon. I can feel Everett looking at me, internally assessing what he might say next.

"What do you know of the future King of Oresteia?"

I huff, annoyance now fueling my tone. "Perhaps too much."

"Ah," he laughs. "I see."

"Do you think…" I stop myself, momentarily thinking better of continuing that sentence. I change my mind last minute, knowing I can trust the brother that sits beside me. "Do you think… someday… I might lend you a hand in ruling the Kingdom? I may not have much to offer, but I will offer you all I have."

Everett puts an arm around my shoulders, pulling me in close. "I think someday, a bridge will need to be built between Paralia and Oresteia once more. I believe you might be the only Frey capable of doing so."

"What if I'm not sure I'd be able to?" I question, my voice caught in my throat.

He kisses the top of my forehead. "When that day comes, if that proves to be true—though I hardly believe that will be the case—we will handle it together."

CHAPTER THIRTY-NINE

The days pass—long and unhurried.

Slowly, I reorient myself back into my routines here. My mornings are filled next to the Neronian, my afternoons spent traveling back and forth between Komeus to see Callious, and I occasionally travel to the gate to listen to gossip circulating concerning the brewing war.

We have not yet heard anything from King Kori regarding his intentions as far as I am aware, and his army at the gate has not advanced any further down the isthmus.

My evenings are accompanied with family dinners and boring conversations. Though there is a nostalgia here of what is familiar, there's still a nagging sense of unease deep within my bones—a feeling that I no longer fit in the world I once called 'home'.

A feeling that maybe I never did.

With hardly a person to talk to, and hours on my hands, I find myself resorting to writing journal pages worth of letters to Will—letters he will surely never read.

> William,
> Did you notice?
> That I can no longer call you 'Will'?
> When we talked of nicknames, you said there is nothing more special than trusting someone enough to allow them to choose a name for yourself.
> It has become clear to me that you do not trust me. I'm not sure if you ever did.
> I held my heart out openly to you from the moment we rode to the stronghold on Agrius' back. Though I knew Kori was not worth my time, I thought that you would be.
> I was mistaken.
>
> William,
> I understand. I understand why you kept Selene's secret. I understand why she took it. I've spent my life longing for more, knowing that it will never come to pass. Then, suddenly, on my birthday of all days, I was given the chance to experience a new world.
> I was terrified.
> But I was also committed. Committed to doing what I could to be helpful and learn what I needed to of your Kingdom and culture.

I could have helped, somehow.

*I wish you would have seen me as an asset
rather than a hindrance.*

William,

*I know you weren't trying to hurt me, but it
feels as though you carved my heart from my
chest. I'm thankful for the day I scarred you
with that rock, because now you have
scarred me.*

William,

I sigh, unable to find the words. Sunlight filters through my sheer curtains, casting a warm glow over the light hardwood floor I lay on. I kick my feet behind me, my head propped on my hand.

I've been laying here for hours, expressing my tumultuous thoughts through hurried, written words.

I pick up my journal, slowly flipping through the pages. I trace a finger over the words on the page, over the curve of his name in ink. A bittersweet smile plays on my lips, my eyebrows crinkled in frustration.

I shut my journal with a snap, trying to shake off the heaviness settling in my chest. Every time I write to William, I am only momentarily able to breathe again before I begin to mourn what could have been again.

I hear Everett out in the hall, his voice booming through the thin wooden door. There's a multitude of voices talking back to him, reminding me that privacy is impossible to come by in this palace.

I wish I had my own Eremos cottage.

I pick myself off of the floor, brushing off my lemon-colored dress.

After tossing my journal on my bed, the lilac covers still in disarray from my night's sleep, I head to my bathroom to freshen up.

The bathroom is filled with soft, diffused light. I gaze at my reflection in the mirror, shocked by the changes I see. My skin, which had begun losing color in Oresteia, is once again darkened by the sun. My cheeks and nose are tinged pink with sunburn, no longer touched by harsh and bitter winds.

My freckles have returned, contrasting once more against my skin.

I lift a hand to my long curls, noticing streaks of sun-bleached color on a few strands.

A pang of sadness hits my heart, feeling as though I have completely erased my time in Oresteia from my physical body within just a few days.

A quick knock interrupts my thoughts, drawing my attention back to my bedroom. Without further notice, Leila enters.

Her short golden curls take after our mother's, bouncing as she glides into my room.

"What are you doing?" She sits on my bed, her blue dress rustling as she crosses her legs underneath.

"What are *you* doing?" I shoot back at her, confused at her sudden appearance.

She looks around my room, avoiding eye contact. "You know, I hardly noticed you were gone."

I snort. "Wow, thank you, Leila, for those kind words." I walk to my door, opening it slightly. "If you'll please be on your way, it appears I have work to do to remind you of my presence."

She rolls her eyes, but gets up, nonetheless. "That's hardly what I meant. Before, you often kept company with only Callious or yourself. It was not often that we saw much of you then, so when you left, it did not feel any different."

I gesture with my hand that she should make her way toward the open door. "It's not as if the hoard of you tried to include me in your daily practices."

As she makes her way to the door, she pauses to look at me. She's a tad bit taller than I am, making it impossible to avoid her eye contact when she stands this close. "We'd like to do things differently this time. That's all I'm attempting to say."

Stunned, I stand behind the door as she exits. She turns to me before walking down the hall, raising her voice. "You have a visitor, by the way. In the greenhouse."

With that, she rotates and leaves me standing here —confused and hopeful for what is to come.

CHAPTER FORTY

I make my way to the front foyer, where my sisters all stand huddled together. Ana and Eva have their arms intertwined as they giggle with Leila in hushed voices.

I see them sneak glances at me as I approach the tall, grand front doors.

"He's handsome," Ana says to me, smiling a knowing smile.

I give her a questioning look but continue on my way without indulging in their conversation.

The sun casts a warm tint over the manicured gardens of our palace. A cobblestone path winds its way through tall paspalos grass, leading to a tall greenhouse nestled in the sand.

The sunlight filters in through the vast windows as I push open the ornate doors to step inside. The air is thick with the scent of flowers, their delicate petals reaching toward the sun streaming in through the glass ceiling.

I wander through the rows of plants, each one meticulously cared for by our gardeners. I trail my fingers over the variety of leaves, making my way toward the back corner where a pink velvet couch awaits.

"Penelope."

My heart stops at the sight of William sitting before me. He abruptly stands, looking as if he might rush over to me in an instant.

I grind my teeth together. "What are you doing here?"

His eyes light up as he takes a step closer to me. Unconsciously, I take a step back. His eyes watch the movement intently, assessing me.

"You forgot these." He reaches toward the couch set behind him, grabbing two books from the soft fabric. He holds them out to me, their covers revealing the two romance books I had taken from the library one day.

My eyes widen in surprise. I never had a chance to read them, as I had forsaken them in the kitchen so we might explore the throne room.

I give him a sideways glance. "I forgot these a while ago."

He shoots me a half-smile, tilting his head to the right in amusement. "I was waiting for the right time."

William sits back on the couch, patting the seat next to him apprehensively.

I roll my eyes, clutching at the books against my chest and follow his bidding.

"So," I begin. "Are you here to proclaim war on Paralia once and for all?"

"On the contrary, I am here to apologize to your father. I would not be surprised, though, if Paralia decides to announce war against us, given all that has happened."

"Your father sent you here to… apologize? That does not sound like the King I know."

William smirks. "He does not know I'm here."

Silence overtakes us—the tension between us palpable.

"It seems as though conflict may be unavoidable," I say.

I'm not talking about our Kingdoms, William.

"It appears so."

I don't think he is, either.

"I do wish there was another way. I hope someday, we might find a peaceful resolution."

"I believe that day might be closer than we think."

We sit in companionable quiet, my heart softening by the minute with his presence.

"Would you like me to accompany you to my father?" I ask.

"There are matters here I'd like to discuss first, if that's acceptable to you."

I nod, unable to stop myself from chewing on my bottom lip in uncertainty.

His gaze is earnest as our eyes meet, and my breath catches in my throat as emotions swirl within me.

"I tried to tell you, Penelope. Twice I was interrupted—once in the heat of our conversation, once by my father. It was not my intention to keep you in the dark, but there was not a good time or place to let you in."

"We were alone my entire last evening. You're saying you could not have told me on Escaeus' peak? While dancing under the stars? In the darkness of my room?"

"I realized it might be my last night with you—I did not want to sully it with accusations and hard conversations. I realize now that was a mistake. I should have tried harder."

"I felt like a fool, William. *You* made me feel like a fool."

"I did. And there is nothing I will not do to make it up to you—to prove to you that I believe you are capable, smart, and better than me in every way. My actions do not correspond correctly with my opinion of you, though I understand what I did speaks louder than what I can say."

William moves to be in front of me, his white pants now stained by the dirt as he kneels.

"I will not beg you to forgive me. I do not deserve to be forgiven by you, nor will I ever be worthy to be seen by you. My father has corrupted me, and I have let him—that I know to be true. But I cannot resist the urge to be drawn to you like a moth to a flame. You are the sun and I the stars—I will never hold a candle to the light you produce."

"This doesn't change how I feel. You see me just as everyone else does—someone incapable and unneeded. I would have been there for her—I would have helped you."

"A fact I recognized much too late." He takes my hands from me sincerely. "You would truly make a remarkable queen, Penelope. You care deeply. You listen intently. You understand what many do not. I…"

I cut him off. "I will never be anyone's queen, William."

"Be mine."

"Will!" I gasp.

"I do not care if you lead my country to ruination, so long as I get to be beside you while you do it. My father's reign is coming to pass—my time growing closer and closer as the days go by. I know I betrayed your trust; I know you have every right to deny me access to your life. But I believe Paralia and Oresteia could live peacefully side by side, and I have confidence that it is *you* that will make that happen."

I nod, his words confirming something in me regarding what Everett and I spoke of days before.

Maybe this is what I'm meant for.

A lull in our conversation gives me room to think, reminding me of the reason this all came to pass.

"Where is Selene?" My tone is serious, my eyebrows furrowed.

William runs a hand through his hair, distressed. "My father denounced her status as royalty. She was sent to Copolis to live and work, banished from joining our royal guard and army. I've gone to see her every day. She is… hurt. But, she is cared for. Father refuses to speak to me about it, no matter how much I push."

I gasp. "She doesn't deserve that."

"She's taking it better than I would be. While I don't agree with my father's reasoning, I do think she will learn to enjoy the independence she is freely receiving. I tried to convince my father to send me with her, but it appears I am stuck as heir."

"When you are king," I begin, "will you let Selene fight?"

He smiles at me, his eyes sparkling. "If she will have it, she will be General."

I laugh softly, amusement filling my chest.

In the solitude of my mind, I allow myself to think back to Will's actions and words in the short time I've known him. My eyes trace the contours of his face as he looks at me.

My wounds are tender, but he is sincere in his apology and reassurance. There is a vulnerability in his tone that I have not yet found in another.

The walls I quickly built around my heart seem to soften, the bricks crumbling by the second as we sit here together.

"I'm still mad at you." I say, though I do not find that to be entirely true anymore.

He releases my hand, holding his own over his heart. "I would rather have your anger than your absence."

CHAPTER FORTY-ONE

As the golden hues of the setting sun paint a sky of woven colors, we sit atop the cliff together, overlooking Paralia. The air is filled with a sense of peace, a tranquility found only after a battle won.

This afternoon, Everett readily affirmed our plans, ecstatic for the promise Will's future reign holds. I am to be leaving with him in the morning, beginning my occupation as ambassador. Though I have much to learn, I am confident I can learn it by the prince's side.

As we gaze at the Kingdom spread out before us, the sea gently lapping at the rugged shore, today's ending feels bittersweet.

My father claimed it would be Paralia's loss to proclaim war against Oresteia, though he did not seem opposed to the idea entirely. He was not thrilled by my declaration to leave, but I have pronounced that's not something he gets to decide. Despite Will's intention to apologize, my father was not impressed by his sudden appearance.

It seems as though the grudge is held both ways and will be for some time longer.

I lay my head on Will's shoulder. Though we do not know what lays ahead for us, I do know we will be able to face it together.

EPILOGUE
PENELOPE

I ONCE BELIEVED THAT TO BE DRAWN TO LIGHT IS TO feel alive.

That to bask in the warmth of the sun is to feel at home.

Until Oresteia.

Before, Paralia had forgone feeling like home. I had longed to experience something new. I begged the sun to hide, so that I might experience the touch of rain on my skin, or the bite of cold air upon my nose.

And yet, the sun did not give in. Day after day, my bright star showed up and asked me to drown in its rays. My only reprieve was the night sky and the coolness that evening brought.

Now here I am, huddled in the warmth of a fire, surrounded by a snowstorm so violent it shakes my windows. I spend my time writing to my siblings of my antics, giving them a glimpse into my life here. Selene and I talk almost daily, taking walks around the city at night with our arms intertwined.

I recharge my soul by sipping on a mug of hot chocolate, lying under a blanket my mother made long ago to symbolize new beginnings.

The sun no longer soaks into my heart and skin, but the memory of its rays will never leave my mind.

Here, with William, I found a place where my soul can run free without the burden of forsaking change.

Here, in Oresteia, I found home.

EPILOGUE
WILLIAM

I will write poems regarding her beauty.

She is the most stunning person I've ever laid eyes on. The golden touch of her skin seeps into my thoughts like a warm summer day. Her brown eyes hold answers to questions I didn't know I needed to ask. Her dark hair wraps around my dreams like a lover's caress. Her laughter flits through my mind like a song on the wind.

After loving her from when I first met her at nine, I cannot believe that Penelope Frey is undoubtedly, wholeheartedly, finally:

mine.

MISSED BOOK TWO?

Want more of these characters? Read *The Dagger's Tide* to explore the other side of Penelope's story. Out everywhere now!

ACKNOWLEDGMENTS

Truthfully, I never thought I would reach this point. When the days were long, and the word count seemed daunting, I convinced myself that it would be fine if the story I was writing stayed right where it was—never to be seen or read by anyone but myself.

Nevertheless, I pushed through, recognizing the deep desire within myself to be able to say I completed this book.

And I did!

This never would have been possible without a multitude of people. Every person I've spoken to about my author-journey has been nothing but encouraging and excited for me.

Even if this is the only book I write in my lifetime, I feel accomplished in knowing I have a village of people who support me and are behind me.

First, I want to thank the Lord for giving me a passion for creative writing and an imagination to follow suite. I have always had a book in my hands, a story to be written in my heart. It is no small thing that in a time of confusion and chaos, writing is what got me through. The talent He has instilled in me is one I will sing His glory of forever.

Second, to my best friend, husband, lover, life partner, teammate, answered prayer, real life book boyfriend: Hunter. Not only have you read every word along the way, but you sing of my story to every person who asks (and even those who don't). You have affirmed me, held me, encouraged me, prodded me, loved me, inspired me. Without you, I never would have finished this, let alone started it. Living this life by your side is the greatest gift I've ever received. Thank you for choosing me. Let's go celebrate with some ice cream.

To Lauren Mebane, a girl who is quite literally half of my own heart. Thank you for editing my book while being busy living your own life. Thank you for being as obsessed with these characters as I am. Mostly, thank you for the way you know me. I've never had a best friend like you.

To Abby Brower, my other editor, grade A yapper, and the best coworker I've ever had. I have you to thank for Chapter 36. When your story gets told, I will be the first one in line for a copy.

My deepest gratitude goes to my family—the ones that raised me and the ones that welcomed me. I'm so blessed to have so many people behind me that are just as excited about this process as I am. Your unwavering love, patience, and intent questions have kept me going throughout.

I know it's a bit uncommon, but I would like to carve out a space to acknowledge myself. When I dreamed of these characters in November of 2023, I never imagined I'd start writing their story in February of 2024, just to finish the novel four months later. I wanted to write a book that I would have loved growing up—one for both 10-year-olds and 40- year-olds alike. I truly believe I've surpassed what I thought I was capable of. What an incredible feeling!

Lastly, to my readers. Knowing you decided to pick up this book blows my mind. Your interest and support mean everything to me. Whether you are here because you know me, or you don't, you are welcome here. Reading is both a safe space and a home to my heart and I hope you find delight and rest in the words of these pages.

I can never thank you enough,
Macayla Dawn

ABOUT THE AUTHOR

Macayla Dawn is a reader first and a writer second.

Growing up, she found herself drawn to worlds filled with demigods, fae, mystery and magic. The characters on those pages became more than just words in a book—they became friends. She is passionate about Jesus, grammar, fantasy, creativity, and ice cream.

In her free time, she loves to read (duh!), write, and explore different ways to express her creativity in all she does. She stays active through tennis, pickleball, working out, and walking with her husband and their dog. She loves to soak up the sun and host gatherings of all sorts.

Originally from Southeast Kansas, she now lives her dream life in Indiana.

Be sure to follow her Instagram and TikTok: @authormacayladawn.

Photograph taken by Hunter Redmon.

ALSO BY MACAYLA DAWN

The Dagger's Tide

Echoes of Elynia